Taking Chances

Rose Marie Meuwissen

Published by
Satin Romance
An Imprint of Melange Books, LLC
White Bear Lake, MN 55110
www.satinromance.com

Taking Chances ~ Copyright © 2015 by Rose Marie Meuwissen

ISBN: 978-1-68046-067-4

Names, characters, and incidents depicted in this book are products of the author's imagination or are used fictitiously. Any resemblance to actual events, locales, organizations, or persons, living or dead, is entirely coincidental and beyond the intent of the author or the publisher. No part of this book may be reproduced or transmitted in any form or by any means, electronic or mechanical, including photocopying, recording, or by any information storage and retrieval system, without permission in writing from the publisher.
Published in the United States of America.

Cover Art by Stephanie Flint

Dedication

To my children, Shane Meuwissen, Tiffany Warford and Cassandra Papin who always encouraged me to pursue my dream of publishing my stories.

To my critique partner, Kathy Nordstrom, who read the first chapter to the last chapter of this story numerous times during the journey of this manuscript.

To Nancy Schumacher who was willing to take a chance on me and my story.

Chapter One

Had she just really been laid off from her job? What else could possibly go wrong? Shana Madden kept asking herself that question.

She was completely alone. Her mother was gone now. Often, she wondered what she would feel like when it happened—when her mother died. She'd anticipated it would be difficult, but never realized it would make such a difference to her everyday life. Death was just so final. Every day she missed her. Missed talking to her on the phone. Hearing her soothing voice telling her everything would be okay.

Shana had been employed in her marketing position at Ultimate Promotions for almost ten years. Moving up the ladder of success, she'd finally landed her dream job. She loved it. Being somewhat of a workaholic, she lived and breathed her job—the ad campaigns and planning marketing events for her clients. So busy working all the time, she hadn't realized how desperately she actually needed the extra money her latest promotion had added to her paycheck. Now the bills for all her mother's extra care, towards the end of her life, began arriving in the mail. The funeral costs were considerably more than she'd ever anticipated. *Who knew it cost nearly $10,000 for a funeral these days?*

The intense shock she felt when she was called into her manager's office earlier today was unimaginable. Roscoe Advertising recently bought out the company. Everyone was reassured there would not be any employment changes and no one needed to be concerned about their jobs.

They lied. Boy, did they lie!

Rose Marie Meuwissen

After the takeover by the new owners, over half of the staff was laid off—including her.

Life certainly sucked. The day simply couldn't get any worse. It was five o'clock and she only had a few more personal things to load into a box as she finished cleaning out her office cubicle. Sadly, ten years of her life fit neatly into one small empty printer-paper box. Unfortunately, that was the sad truth of her career. Did she actually have anything of value to show for the past ten years? Probably not. Only memories. The happy ones she would always remember, but that was about it. Just a few memories and one box to take with her.

She should probably be on the brink of tears at this point, but they didn't seem to be coming. Only a couple of stray tears managed to slide down her cheek in the past hour. Her co-workers stopped by one by one to say how sorry they were and reassure her everything would be okay. She'd be able to start over with a different company and probably be paid a higher salary. Nonetheless, she could sense the relief in their voices that it hadn't been them. *They still had jobs, so of course they could say everything would be okay.*

Truth of the matter was she wouldn't be anywhere near okay unless she got a new job tomorrow. There were already way too many bills to pay. She barely earned enough money to pay them with a steady paycheck and there definitely wouldn't be enough now. Any way you looked at it, she was now in deep financial trouble.

Mother was sick for over a year before her death, just three months ago, and Shana had agreed to pay the nursing home bills. *What other choice did she have?* After all, it was her mother, the only family she'd had left. She had no brothers or sisters to help and her dad died years ago. No, it was only her. She was responsible for taking care of her mother's affairs so she promised to make payments. Eventually, it would get paid off. No matter how long it took, she would do it. Unfortunately, it really helped to have a job. Oh, she'd file for unemployment, but the checks would barely be enough to cover the essentials.

Shana picked up the box, her organizer bag and purse, then stopped and turned back for a second to stare at the cubicle she'd called home for the last ten years. Another tear slid down her cheek as she proceeded down the hall and headed for the door.

It really wasn't very far to her car in the parking lot, although it seemed like the longest walk of her life. She got in and sat serenely in the driver's seat, blankly staring out the windshield. Reaching into her purse, she pulled out her cell phone and started to call her mother. Then abruptly stopped. It was a habit to always call her mother on her drive home from work. She ended the call as her heart broke into a million pieces and tears rolled down her cheeks. She was so alone. The feeling of hopelessness was overwhelming.

"You'll be okay. Get a grip girl." *Now she was even talking to herself. Only crazy people did that, didn't they?*

Shana knew she should go home, but couldn't. She didn't have any idea where to go but knew she needed to be around people. Driving without a destination definitely was not a good thing. She ended up in the parking lot of Bear Creek Pass, a local Minneapolis eating and drinking establishment catering to the career people after work. She couldn't remember going through any intersections or even getting off the freeway. *A very scary thought.*

Having a drink seemed like the appropriate thing to do in this situation. The only problem was she didn't drink. Maybe, one on rare occasions. Most people thought drinking solved all their problems, so this would be as good a time as any to try out the theory. For drinking to have any affect, more than one drink undoubtedly was needed, and one was usually her limit. It was worth trying it out tonight. The theory. She had no place else to go and didn't have to go to work in the morning. *What could it hurt?*

She hated going to bars, especially alone. She walked in and sat down on a high stool at the bar. It wasn't crowded yet, however probably would be soon. It was happy hour, so she ordered a frozen strawberry margarita, which unfortunately, or fortunately, depending on how you looked at it, meant she would get two, and a chicken fingers appetizer.

She'd been so busy working on her Dallas event for Holiday Travel; she never took the time to have lunch. She skipped lunch many times and worked straight through the day. She was dedicated to her job and her career. What a fool she'd been! It didn't matter to her company. Not one bit. They completely managed to get the work of two people out of her for the price of one. They weren't the fools in this one, she was. At her next job, she was going to take lunch every day, no matter what.

The strawberry margarita was cool and refreshing. The first one was gone along with half of the chicken and she was halfway finished with her second drink. Well, she hadn't eaten all day after all. The bartender asked if she would like another drink. She looked up at him, trying to concentrate on what he was saying. It had gotten very loud. She looked around the bar and realized it was almost full except for the bar stool next to her. The bartender was still waiting for her answer. She nodded. What the Hell. It was only two drinks and she had eaten so she should be okay to have another one.

Music was now playing and the lights were lower. She noticed people were out dancing and having a good time. Must be nice.

"Would you like to dance?"

Her mind was clouded, but she thought someone was talking to her. Something about dancing? She looked up to see a breathtakingly handsome man waiting for her reply.

"It's only a dance."

"Uh, oh sure." *I don't have anything to lose, do I?* She got up off the stool and swayed slightly. Then walked to the dance floor with him following.

She danced and moved her body to the beat of the music, swinging her hips seductively and tossing her long blond hair from side to side. She looked up at him and smiled. He was just under six feet tall, trim and fit. His body glowed with a natural tan from the sun. He grinned down at her with appreciation as he watched her dance. She moved closer to him dancing even more seductively than before.

The dancing proved to be the right thing. It made her forget about her problems and allowed her body to relax, of course the alcohol probably helped, too. They danced to a couple of songs and then headed back to the barstools.

"Sorry, I didn't introduce myself, I'm Kal," he said extending his hand.

Taking Chances

"Shana," she said shaking his hand.

"Mind if I join you at the bar?" he asked.

"No, of course not."

"I'd order you a drink but it looks like you're set," he said looking at two strawberry margaritas in front of her.

"Happy hour." She always hated this part, trying to make conversation with a stranger. He certainly was good looking, unfortunately, that usually meant he either had a girlfriend or didn't want one. You could tell he worked out by the muscles in his arms and his flat stomach. His hair was coal black, cut in a short business style, and his eyes were baby blue. Hell he probably had women falling at his feet to get dates with him. What was he doing talking to her? Probably was having an off night and wanted to score tonight for a one-night stand. Well, he just may be in luck. One-night stands were not her style, in fact, she'd never had one, nonetheless, tonight she just didn't really care. If she ever needed to be close to someone, it was tonight. The thought of being held in his arms, even for a few hours was immensely appealing. She was jumping the gun though, because he hadn't actually hinted towards sleeping with her at all, yet she sure as hell was thinking about it.

"So what do you do?" he asked.

"I'm in advertising," she answered, not exactly lying yet not actually getting into the truth of the matter that as of today she didn't have a job. "And you?" she countered to take the focus off her.

"I'm in the medical field," he said not really offering more. "This is a good song. Would you like to dance again?"

"Sure," she answered, getting up off the stool. It was a slow one. Usually she didn't dance slow ones with strangers, however she didn't want to talk about jobs and she wanted to feel his hard body pressed against hers.

* * * *

Kal took her in his arms and pressed her tightly against him. She felt good, he thought. It had been a year since he'd broken up with his fiancée—rather she had broken up with him. He hadn't felt like going out for a long time, but tonight he was feeling lonely and wanted some female companionship. Even if it was only for one night. She smelled good, some type of musk, he decided. Her hair felt like silk as he ran his fingers through the long strands hanging down her back. Her body was soft and yielding—it had been so long since he'd allowed himself the pleasure of a woman's company, or body for that matter.

The band played two slow songs in a row. He enjoyed every minute of them. When the second one ended, he bent his head and kissed her lips as she looked up at him. Nice. Very nice, he thought as he pulled away. They walked back to their barstools and he ordered them each another drink. He sensed she was about over her limit; still he wanted to go home with her tonight. He knew it was wrong, because Hell, he didn't even know her, yet he knew she was what he wanted tonight and it had been way too long.

"Do you watch football? The Vikings aren't doing very well, as usual."

"Sometimes. I've been to a couple of games." She welcomed the non-relevant conversation of sports that went on for quite a while.

They talked, they drank, they danced, until the bar was ready to close.

"I'll walk you to your car," he offered and took her arm to lead her outside. When they got to her five-year-old black Kia Elantra, he turned her around into his arms and kissed her lips again, and then moved to her neck and up to her ear. He whispered, "I'd like to come home with you, if you are interested."

Shana looked up at him. "I thought you'd never ask. It's not far from here. You can follow me."

Kal walked to his two-year-old red Corvette and got in. He pulled up behind her and followed her to her apartment. He questioned the wisdom of his actions during the drive, though his body was ready and he knew he needed to be with her tonight. It wouldn't go any further than that, a one-night stand, but that was okay.

* * * *

Shana led him into her small apartment, turned on the stereo to the Smooth Jazz station and turned the lights down low. She was going to do this; nevertheless, she did want to be seduced first. After all, there was no need to rush. She sat down on the couch where he joined her. *Wow, this seemed awkward.*

"You are a very beautiful woman, Shana." He brushed her hair off her shoulder, began kissing her neck and moved slowly to her lips. She kissed him back. He stood and pulled her up off the couch to slow dance with him. He wrapped her in his arms and pressed her against his body. His hands roamed down her back to her butt and he pulled her even closer. She could feel him pressing against her body. She turned so her back was now pressed against his chest. He put his hand on her stomach and slid his hand up underneath her blouse to caress her breast.

Shana gasped. It felt so good and it had been so very long. Over two years ago. No man had touched her since the divorce from a marriage that only lasted a year. She took his hand and led him to the bedroom. She pulled back the comforter and sheet and then undressed. Kal did the same. It seemed so weird to be doing this with someone she didn't know. Thank heavens it was dark in the room and her whole thinking process was clouded by all the alcohol. She got into the bed. Seconds later Kal was lying naked beside her, kissing her eager lips again, blissfully allowing her to forget everything except the wonderful sensations spiraling throughout her body from his hungry lips. Kisses that threatened to devour her. She was on fire and ready for him. Hell, she'd been ready all night.

Kal was about to enter her body when a moment of reality flashed in her mind to remind him to use a condom. Then she decided to hell with it, rolled over on top of him, and slid down on his rock hard erection, covering him completely with her body. He felt so damn good! She felt his reluctance, but soon they both were overtaken by a sexual frenzy escalating between them and she didn't give protection another thought. He rolled over on top of her then and finished quickly as they climaxed together. The last thing she remembered was Kal apologizing for finishing so soon before she passed out from sheer mental and physical exhaustion mixed with way too much alcohol.

* * * *

Kal woke up at five the next morning. He looked at the woman lying in bed next to him still asleep. Last night he'd had great sex with her even though she'd obviously had a little too much to drink. At this time in his life, he didn't want to get involved and hadn't mentioned anything about looking for a relationship. Yesterday had been a bad day. Hell, he'd had a bad year. Sometimes, a guy simply needed a woman. This was only for one night. He dressed quietly so he wouldn't wake her. He felt bad though, so he pulled out a fifty-dollar bill and placed it on the table with a note.

Thanks for a wonderful night. Use this to buy something for yourself. Kal.

He closed the door quietly and left. His flight left at seven. It was a good thing he packed yesterday so everything was ready to go. The conference he was attending was in Atlanta and he would be gone for almost a week. *Probably was best for both of them.*

* * * *

Shana woke up about seven the next morning with a headache, that wouldn't quit. Finally, she sat up, desperately knowing she needed some Tylenol. She looked over at the other side of her king size bed and remembered someone had been lying there with her last night.

"Oh, shit!" she said as she quickly reached for her aching head. Where was he? She got up and walked to the living room. The apartment was deathly quiet. *He must've left without even saying good-bye.* She made it to the kitchen to get a bottle of water out of the refrigerator and the Tylenol from the cupboard. On the counter, she saw a fifty-dollar bill and a note. She read the note and looked at the money. Damn. She actually started to laugh.

This was her first one-night stand, so she wasn't exactly sure, although she didn't think you were supposed to get paid for it. *Were you? Did he think I was a hooker?* Oh well, she certainly could use the money although she was certain she'd behaved like a wanton woman since she'd drank more than her usual one drink, so she didn't actually care. She didn't want to see him ever again. Not that the sex wasn't good. Because from what she recalled, it was pretty damned good. They definitely had chemistry! Besides, she would be far too embarrassed to see him again.

Taking Chances

Vaguely she remembered him saying he had a flight to catch in the morning and he would be gone for a week. That would work out just fine, because she'd given him her business card. The card for the job she didn't have anymore, so he wouldn't be able to get ahold of her there. Thankfully, she'd already given her one-month notice on her apartment because she would be moving to her mother's small apartment this weekend for the time being anyway. At least until she found a new job and figured out what she was going to do with her life now.

Chapter Two

"Last box!" Shana said as she put the label on the box in front of her. She sat back and looked at the stack of boxes lined up against the wall in the bedroom. She'd been living in her mom's apartment for three months now and still had to dodge boxes to get from room to room. Finally, she had all of her mother's things sorted out. Throwing her mom's things away had been extremely difficult because she hated to throw perfectly good things away. You never knew when you might need the stuff, like when you were completely flat broke. Which would be right now.

She had sat on the floor, gone through drawers and boxes, and cried. It was almost like watching a movie of her life, as the memories of her childhood in vivid color pictures flashed in front of her eyes. Pictures of her and her mother. Then the tears would flow freely and she had to put every ounce of energy into focusing so she could finish the box or drawer. One per day was all she'd been able to manage. Which was why she was finally done, three months later.

There were three stacks of boxes. One to throw away, one to sell at the area garage sale and one to keep. They were all stacked in her mother's bedroom. She slept in the guest room, because she couldn't bring herself to sleep in her mother's room. It felt too weird. At least not for now anyway.

There were also a couple of rows of Shana's boxes stacked alongside of her mother's. She'd only unpacked her clothes and the necessities, because she wasn't sure how long she'd be staying. The rent was low compared to what else was out there, but she still hadn't found a job. Granted she hadn't been looking too hard. She didn't have

Taking Chances

any drive left. After everything she'd been through recently, she was depressed. Under the circumstances, who wouldn't be? She wasn't too worried about it, except it sure did zap your energy. She did manage to send out or email five resumes per week. That was her goal and she'd stuck to it. Out of all the ones she sent out, she'd only received about five interviews. None of them seemed right for her. Of course, nothing seemed right anymore at all. Thank God for unemployment checks! People were always complaining about how the government just gave money away. Well, that's probably because they'd never needed to use it. Well, she sure needed it. About all it covered was the rent, utilities, her car payment and car insurance. Good thing she didn't eat much because there was very little left over for groceries. Actually, she hadn't been feeling so great lately. Besides feeling depressed, she wasn't hungry and the thought of food, made her feel nauseous. Unfortunately, she hadn't been able to pay the Cobra payments to keep up her medical insurance, so she couldn't afford to go see the doctor. Besides, with everything she'd been through, she was sure it was only depression.

She heard knocking and got up to answer the door. She looked through the peephole. It was her neighbor. She opened the door and said, "Hi, Sam."

"Shana, how are you doing?" he asked.

"Okay, I guess."

"Still going through boxes, huh?"

"It's a slow, sad process, unfortunately," she stated, looking back towards the last box sitting on the floor.

"I know …" he paused, "I know all too well. It took me awhile to get going after my Ellie passed on." He handed her a container.

"What is it?"

"I made my special recipe chili. It makes a lot, so I thought maybe you might like some."

"Thank you, Sam. That's very kind of you."

"Thought maybe you could use some. I know when you've lost someone special, you don't feel much like cooking or eating. Right?"

"As a matter of fact, I haven't felt much like eating at all lately. Hadn't really thought about it though as to why."

"I know it's hard, yet you have to go on with your life without her. You're still young, and you're here. God has a purpose for you." He paused. "Sorry. You don't need to be lectured by some old man. Promise me you'll try my special recipe chili. I'm quite proud of it."

"Actually, I haven't eaten today. I promise to taste it. Thank you."

Sam started walking away, but stopped and turned back. "Let me know what you think of it."

Shana shut the door and walked into the kitchen. The minute she took the cover off, she could smell the rich tomato base. She loved chili and it smelled great. Her stomach lurched and she went running for the bathroom, barely making it to the toilet. She didn't throw up much because she hadn't eaten anything. *What was that all about?* It certainly wasn't the chili because she hadn't even gotten to take a bite.

It took two more weeks of the queasy stomach before Shana realized what should've been obvious. She knew she'd missed her period the last two months, but had discounted it to the stress of losing her mother, job and apartment. Stress can do that. However, she had conveniently chosen to forget her one-night stand with unprotected sex. When the reality of her situation sunk in, she practically ran to her car and drove like a maniac to Walgreen's to buy a pregnancy test. She hoped it wasn't a waste of money, although on the other hand, she wished it were. *How crazy is that?*

Not sure if she truly wanted to know one way or the other, she still rushed home. In the bathroom she read the instructions twice to make sure she did it right. The minutes passed slowly in the silent bathroom as she reminded herself to breathe. Several moments later, Shana stared at the results, not believing what she saw. She was pregnant!

"Shit!" was all she could say as she slid to the floor slowly and hung her head over the edge of the bathtub. She cried and cried and cried until there wasn't a drop left in her. She finally managed to walk to the bedroom. She laid down on her big, king-sized bed and curled in a ball with her knees against her chest. The last thing she remembered before falling asleep was pulling the comforter over her traitorous body.

Shana couldn't force herself to get up. She just lay in the bed as her body kept reminding her mind she was pregnant. The queasiness of

Taking Chances

her stomach was definitely a reminder. She knew she had to eat something except how was she supposed to do that when the mere thought of eating made her feel like vomiting? She struggled to get up and made it to the kitchen to find some saltine crackers.

Thankfully, she had some Sprite on hand, because she always had some for flu emergencies. A few hours later, she was feeling a little better, so she decided to try some chicken noodle soup. She kept a few cans on hand for just this type of occasion—when she came down with the flu. It was a good thing she got some food down because she was feeling light headed too. She grabbed a quilt and sat down on the couch to watch TV. She needed to get her mind off the whole pregnancy thing.

It worked for a while, however then her thoughts drifted back to the pregnancy. Her mind raced. She thought about Kal and their one-night stand. *What were the odds you could get pregnant from doing it once?* Pretty slim, she'd guess. Then if it were going to happen to anyone, it would be her because she certainly wasn't lucky. She wondered if he'd even given her a second thought after he left that morning, or if he had called her old work number or gone to her work.

She hadn't talked to anyone from work since she left that day. It's strange but when you work with people every day, talk to them, eat with them, share details of your lives; you think they're your friends, although they really aren't. You don't do things with them outside of work hours except for work functions. That should be a sign they aren't real friends. However, you have to work together and get along so everyone is nice to each other. It's kind of like being fake friends. Not one called her after she'd been laid off. Not one! Some had known her situation. Her money problems. About her mom. Yet, not one called to see how she was doing or if she'd gotten a new job.

Of course, she hadn't made it easy for anyone to be her friend, either. Not because she didn't want to be friends, merely because she had been over extended with her time between the long hours at work and spending every free moment with her mom. There hadn't been any time left for her, let alone for friends. So now, there was no one she could call to talk to. No one to tell about the pregnancy. No one to talk to about what she should do.

And Kal. She hadn't even gotten his phone number or business card. Of course, she hadn't planned to ever talk to him again so what would she have needed it for. He seemed like a nice person except for the small fact that he got her pregnant.

They should've used protection. They should've used a condom. No. *He* should've used a condom. It's the guy's responsibility. Never mind the fact that she'd been the one to basically sit on his penis. Well, he could've stopped her. Right? Of course, he could've. He could certainly have stopped before he came anyway. That would've helped and then she wouldn't be in this mess.

Well, it wasn't his problem, it was hers. She had no idea where he lived or worked. Hell, she didn't even know what his last name was. So there was no way he was ever going to know what happened. That she had gotten pregnant from their one-night stand. Life just plain sucked. And for her, it hadn't only not gotten better; it had gotten really bad. There was no one to help her, either. No one!

Six hours after Shana got out of bed, she headed to the bedroom and crawled back into bed. There wasn't anything she could do except feel sorry for herself. She cried until she fell asleep because her body was drained, both physically and emotionally. Sleep offered peace. A time when her mind shut down and she no longer had to think about all her problems.

Shana woke the next morning and pretty much went through the same routine. This went on for weeks. She only went out once to buy some groceries and mail some bills.

A month later, she decided to go to a free women's health clinic, Lake Nokomis Health Center. Shana had never been to a free clinic, but then, she'd always had insurance. It wasn't in the best area of the city, however, that was probably because it was in an area people lived in who didn't have insurance or money. The women in the lobby were not dressed well. It was obvious they didn't have money. The kids were dressed in torn clothes or clothes that were either too big or too small. The kids had runny noses and coughs. She was actually afraid to sit down on the chair because she was sure the germs were running rampart in the waiting room.

Taking Chances

They were a sorry bunch of people seated in the waiting room. Probably all on public assistance and here she was. *What did that say?* Shana wanted nothing more than to get up and walk out the door. Only she was just as bad off as the rest of them. She couldn't afford to go anywhere else so she waited her turn.

Her mind went crazy and painted a horrible picture of what her life could be like if she had a baby and no money. That was the sad reality of her situation. No matter how bad her situation was, she had always wanted to have children someday. There simply wasn't any way she could have a baby right now. She didn't have any medical insurance. It cost money to go to the hospital and deliver a baby. She had neither money nor insurance. The baby would have no insurance either.

She had no job. She was too depressed to go look for a job. Hell, she looked depressed. Any Human Resources person would take one look at her depressed state and the interview would be over. She couldn't even take care of herself anymore, so she certainly couldn't take care of a baby.

There just wasn't any way she could do this. She had never agreed with abortion nevertheless now she understood why women in dire circumstances did it. Not all were in dire circumstances though; some simply didn't want to deal with it, regardless. No matter what her thoughts on abortion were, dire circumstances were going to be a huge factor in her case.

* * * *

About a week later, she received a call from the health center.
"Shana?"
"Yes," Shana answered.
"I'm Jane, a nurse from Lake Nokomis Health Center. I'm calling to advise you there was a child in the office on the day of your appointment who was diagnosed with German measles a week later. So you may have come in contact with the virus. Since you are pregnant, it is very important to watch for any symptoms, as the German measles can be very harmful to your unborn baby."

Rose Marie Meuwissen

How could she be so unlucky? She knew that waiting room had been filled with germs, however, German measles she would not have expected.

The nurse continued, "Complications your baby could have, if you came down with the German measles, would be that the baby could be born blind, deaf, have heart defects or brain damage. The chances would be a 50/50 chance."

She just wasn't a lucky person, so if she got it, the baby would probably be born with one or all of those birth defects. There was no doubt in her mind.

"You need to watch closely for any symptoms," the nurse said. "They may not show up right away. If you start running a mild fever or see any signs of a rash consisting of flat pink spots starting on the chest and then spreading to the face, arms and legs, you should call the health center immediately. The rash spots may merge together making the skin look flushed."

Shana wasn't sure what kind of measles she had when she was young and she couldn't ask her mother, so she was just going to assume she'd already had the German measles and not worry about it. Right?

"The incubation period is 14-21 days," the nurse said. "So you only have two weeks to go."

She didn't have a fever or any rash so far. Although there was still time for them to show up. Just what she needed, one more thing about which to be depressed.

For Shana, the next two weeks passed slowly. Each day she got up in the morning and checked for spots. Each day there were none. Finally, she reached the two-week mark. *Could her luck be changing finally?* She was actually excited about that chance. Little did she know how foolish she was to even entertain the thought.

Two days later, she was feeling a little bit under the weather and thought she might be coming down with a cold, not even giving the measles thing a second thought. Then one day later, she stepped out of the shower and while wiping off in front of the mirror saw a sprinkling of spots on her chest. Shana literally stared at herself in the mirror, dropping the towel to the floor. She knew at that moment she had come down with German measles. Now she remembered the nurse said during the first seven days, there would be little or no signs except maybe a mild fever. That was why she hadn't felt up to par the last week. She had been focused on the spots. Forcing herself to put her robe on, she walked to the bed before she collapsed.

She lay on the bed staring at the ceiling fan. At that moment, she knew her life was over. She'd barely been making it through each day the way it was. She was depressed and they couldn't give her anything because she was pregnant. She spent her days crying mostly and had to literally force herself to eat. She wasn't hungry because of her depression and the smell of food made her nauseous from the pregnancy. *So who would want to eat?*

The tears rolled slowly down her flushed cheeks and then ran freely as if a dam had broken loose. She cried for herself, and her and Kal's unborn child. The thought of Kal made her anger rise. This was all his fault! First, he should never have had sex with her without using a condom! It's the guy's responsibility to bring the condom, put it on and use it. What kind of a guy was he anyway? She hadn't a clue. Hell, she didn't even know his last name much less who he was. What kind of guy goes home with a woman he just met in a bar? Who obviously was drunk and had unprotected sex with her. And, to top it all off, sneaks out in the morning, leaving a note with money as if he was paying her for sex. Did he think she was a hooker or what? Hell, she didn't care. The pregnancy was her problem, her mess and she would take care of it.

Shana reached for the phone and called the nurse at the clinic. She knew she had to have someone look at her to confirm she indeed did have German measles. How that was going to happen she wasn't quite sure. She knew she was contagious, so if she went anywhere, she was putting other people at risk. The nurse put her on hold to retrieve her file. When she came back on the line, she informed her a doctor would come to examine her today. She was not to go out or have any contact with anyone. Shana hung up the phone and stared out the window.

She finally got up and dressed. She made a piece of toast and barely managed to get it down with a glass of orange juice. Her life certainly hadn't turned out the way she'd thought it would. She couldn't even recall another time in her life when she'd been depressed. This just wasn't her.

She had been full of life and plans for her future. Except, parents got old and died. That was simply what happened. Only her parents hadn't been that old. They had recently retired and were planning to enjoy their golden years. Then Dad died in a car accident. It just wasn't fair! Mom took it hard. They'd been together for 35 years. Mom lost her will to go on and then she got sick. Then Mom was gone only three years after Dad. That almost threw her into a depression, nonetheless she fought it hard, but when she lost her job, it pushed her to the edge. That alone didn't do it though. It was this unexpected, unintentional, unplanned and unwanted pregnancy.

It wasn't that she didn't want to have a child ever, just not now, like this. Alone. That was the problem; she was alone, so very alone. When she had a baby, she wanted it to be as a result of a loving relationship. And yes, she wanted to have a wedding and a husband first. That was how it was supposed to be and that was what she wanted. She wanted to be healthy, too. Being depressed wasn't healthy and having the German measles wasn't good for her or the baby.

The phone rang. It was the clinic calling to say the doctor would be there any minute. About fifteen minutes later Dr. Satari arrived. Shana was grateful they sent a woman doctor.

After checking Shana over, Dr. Satari said, "Shana you do indeed have the German measles and should not be around anyone who hasn't had them since you are highly contagious still. You should stay home for the next week and after that, you should be over them. Probably would be best to have a family member who's had the German measles before come and stay with you or at least bring you some meals."

Shana didn't say anything. What was she supposed to say? She didn't have any family much less any friends who could help her.

Dr. Satari continued, "Come in for a check-up in two weeks." She walked to the door and left.

Shana walked to the window and stared out at the bright sunshine and the trees now shades of red and orange. It was a beautiful Indian summer day in October. A warm breeze gently blew across her face as she stepped out onto the patio deck. Good thing she stopped at the

Taking Chances

grocery store after her visit to the clinic last week. It had been dollar days at the grocery store, so she stocked up on soup and frozen TV dinners with the little money she had. She wasn't in the least bit hungry; still she would try to get a little of something down each day for the sake of the baby.

"Hello," Shana said as she picked up the ringing phone.

"This is Sam, next door. It was such a lovely day so I went to my friend's apple orchard and I've brought you a bag of apples. I'll be right over." Before she could reply, he hung up.

"Great!" Shana said. *Now what was she to do?* The doorbell rang and she opened it only slightly and said," I've come down with the German measles and am still contagious, so if you set them down by the door, I'll get them."

"Oh, Shana, I'm sorry to hear that. I'm pretty sure I've had them although you never know, so I'll leave the bag here. Hope you enjoy them and hope you feel better soon." With that, Sam headed down the hallway back to his apartment.

"Thanks, Sam. I appreciate you bringing the apples for me," she said as she opened the door to retrieve the bag of apples. Well, now she had apples to go with her soup and TV dinners. It would be a long week that was for sure.

The week passed slowly and so did the next week. However, they did pass and she was on her way to the clinic for her post German measles checkup. She dreaded going into the waiting room, thinking about what happened the last time. This time, however, she was shown to a room immediately. Guess they didn't want to take any chances with her coming down with something else.

Shortly after, Dr. Satari came in. She checked Shana over, thoroughly. Then she became very quiet as though she was in deep thought. She chose her words carefully. "Shana, I want you to know there are strong possibilities your baby will be born with defects because of the German measles. A baby born with any of these possible side effects such as heart or brain damage would require endless amounts of medical attention. To someone without medical insurance, the bills would be astronomical. Deafness and blindness can also occur, which are less dangerous nonetheless still would require increased medical expenses. I have never been an advocate of abortion, although as your doctor, I must advise you of all the possible defects and what impact they will have on you both medically and financially. Much less the emotional impact of dealing with these issues, should they occur."

"Are you advising me to have an abortion?" Shana asked.

"No. It must be your decision. Given your emotional status and the high risk of giving birth to a baby with disabilities, possibly even multiple defects, would be a huge undertaking to someone in good health with insurance and family to help. Of which you have neither."

"Do you do them here?"

"No, however I can give you the name and number of a clinic that does," Dr. Satari offered.

"But, isn't it too late in the pregnancy?"

"No. Not anymore. They can do them right up to the end, although I wouldn't recommend waiting that long."

"Oh," Shana said.

"You go home and think about it. If you have any questions, just call me," Dr. Satari said and handed Shana two business cards. One for the Meadow Brook Center for Women and one of her business cards. Then, she left the room.

Shana sat in the chair a few minutes trying to absorb what Dr. Satari had just said. She was so screwed! She couldn't win no matter what she did. If she killed the baby with an abortion, did she really deserve to live? Maybe they both would be better off dead. Had she actually just thought that? That was a suicide thought. The bad thing was it actually sounded like a good solution to her problems. Hell, then she wouldn't have to deal with any of her problems anymore, and no one would miss her.

Shana rested her head in her hands. This was so not like her. She never thought like this. She needed to be on some anti-depression medication before she did something to end the misery herself. This idea of an abortion may be the solution to her problems. Her health was at stake here. No not her health, on the contrary her life. The sad truth was she was not emotionally strong enough to deal with the emotional or financial strain a baby with defects would put on her. She couldn't even deal with her own emotional and financial problems. The answer

Taking Chances

was clear; she had no other choice except to have an abortion. She would give herself a week to think about it. If she hadn't changed her mind, she would make an appointment at the Meadow Brook Center for Women.

Shana wiped at her eyes. A few tears had managed to slide down her cheeks. She stood and walked out of the room, down the hall and out to her car. Thankfully, it was raining because it suited her gloomy outlook on life, perfectly.

The next day, the weather turned wintery. The sky was overcast and light snowflakes flurried in the air. Winter was coming. She never liked driving in the snow, especially early in the morning to go to work. At least, she didn't have to be anywhere.

The week had passed slowly. And then another. The baby was moving around and she could feel it kick every once in a while. Now realizing it was really a baby inside her made her feel even worse. Thoughts of suicide came more often now. That more than anything made her dial the number for the Meadow Brook Center for Women to make an appointment for next week.

Well, today was the day. It was cold, only 30 degrees, so she bundled up. Thankfully, the apartment building had underground parking. She drove to the Meadow Brook Center for Women, which wasn't far away.

Shana hadn't known before that abortion clinics even existed in the suburbs. It didn't take long to get there, as it was only a few blocks away. The receptionist promptly showed her to a room down a long hallway. Shana's heart was racing. Never in her life had she expected to be in an abortion clinic. She was probably going to Hell for this. Then again, if she committed suicide, she was going to Hell for sure. So here she was. It seemed like an eternity before the doctor came in.

"Hi, I'm Dr. Kessler," he said looking into her eyes. "Why are you here?"

"I've decided to end my pregnancy."

"Why, may I ask?"

"I got pregnant from a one-night stand with a stranger I met in a bar about six months ago. I lost my dad in a car accident three years ago. I lost my mother to cancer about nine months ago. I lost my job almost six months ago, along with my medical insurance. I am depressed to the point of suicide and need to be on medication, which I can't take because I'm pregnant. And if that isn't enough, I came down with German measles about a month ago."

"I see," Dr. Kessler said as he studied Shana. "Do you have any reservations about the abortion at all?"

"My only concern is if God will forgive me for killing my baby." Shana paused to look at Dr. Kessler directly as if he should know the answer. "Enough is enough. I can't take anymore and I don't want to die."

"What do you mean?"

"Suicide is constantly on my mind."

"I see," he said. "I'll send my nurse in to take your vitals and medical history and then I'll do a pelvic exam. Then we'll set up an appointment for next Friday."

"Okay."

"I want you to know that since you are so far along the recovery time will be similar to a normal delivery. So plan on about three to five days. I will give you a prescription for an anti-depressant. You can start taking them three days after the abortion."

"I don't have any insurance so if you could prescribe a generic one or the cheapest one, I would be very appreciative."

"That's right. Let me see if I can get you a couple month's supply of samples."

"Thank you."

"The nurse will go over what you can expect at the abortion," Dr. Kessler stated and left the room.

Shana listened while the nurse explained the procedures for an abortion. The possibility that a C-section might be needed. And the need for a driver to drive her home. If she didn't have one, they could call a volunteer driver to take her home. *What a relief that was.*

Finally, the appointment was over. She walked down the hallway back to the waiting room to leave and noticed the Thanksgiving Day decorations and the sign stating they would be closed on Thursday and Friday for the holiday. She'd forgotten it was Thanksgiving Day on

Taking Chances

Thursday. She would be home alone however she did have a frozen Turkey dinner she could make and pretend it was a fabulous dinner.

Only one more week. She slowly walked to her car. Yes, it was almost over, this horrible nightmare. She had a lot of faith that if she could get through this depression, she could have her life back. Well, not her old life back, but maybe a new and improved life. She had just one more week to go.

* * * *

Dr. Kal Paxton arrived early at the clinic. He didn't know why he let his friend, Dr. John Kessler, talk him into this. John knew he wasn't an advocate of abortion, nonetheless still had managed to persuade him into filling in for him at the clinic today. John had an emergency and had to leave town unexpectedly last night. John's mother was in the hospital after suffering a stroke, so he was flying out to Boston this morning. John was his best friend though and that was what you did, you helped each other. They'd been buddies in med school and always were there for each other, and John had been there for him through his break up with Dana. That's why he was here today.

Kal sat in John's office and looked at the two files for the patients he was taking care of today. Kal's nurse, Jennifer, popped her head in the door to let him know she had made it in to help. She was a doll. Even at the last minute, like today, she'd dropped everything and changed her plans to assist him. Jennifer was in her fifties and had many years of nursing experience in various fields. Her loyalty to him as a doctor was unfailing. She was always there to help out and he could trust her impeccably.

Kal picked up the first file. It was a young woman, only 18, who had been raped by her uncle. She was three months along. Well, this one was understandable at least. He wouldn't have a problem performing this abortion at all. He hoped the uncle had been punished for doing this to a young girl. It would leave her with emotional scars that would last all her life. The procedure would be easy, too.

Kal picked up the second file. A 28-week abortion. He didn't like this at all. The baby would be able to survive on its own. And he would have to kill it. This he wasn't so sure he could do. They most likely would have to cancel this one. *Who would wait until they were this far along to abort a baby?* He flipped to the next page where John had written his notes. The mother, age 30, had been diagnosed with German measles and there was a good chance, almost fifty percent or more, the baby would have some sort of defects. He turned to the next page and saw it was labeled: Her story. That was odd, even though sometimes doctors wrote down what the patients gave as explanations for their predicaments. There wasn't a place for it on the sheets, so it was done this way. Kal was curious so he read on.

Patient states she met a man at a bar a little over six months ago and had unprotected sex. Lost her father in a car accident, her mother to cancer only recently and has no other family. Lost her job about six months ago and has no medical insurance. Severely depressed to the point of suicidal thoughts. Can't be put on any medication due to the pregnancy. Caught German measles from the free clinic she was going to for her prenatal visits.

His mind was whirling. *It couldn't be, could it?* He closed the file to look at her name. Shana Madden. Kal set the file down and pulled out his wallet. He opened it and pulled out the business card he'd been given six months ago. It read: Shana Madden. *It's her. This is her file.*

"Shit!" Kal shouted. *It was his baby. His. He knew it.* He couldn't and wouldn't kill his own child.

Chapter Three

"Everything okay in here?" Jennifer asked, as she opened the door and came in, closing the door behind her.

"No," Kal said. "Definitely not okay." He searched her face, knowing this was someone he could confide in. "Remember the woman I met at the bar over six months ago and couldn't get a hold of? I called her work and she was no longer employed there. Then I went to her apartment and she'd moved. They said they couldn't give me her forwarding address. This is her," he said, handing her the file.

Jennifer looked at the name on the file and opened it to read the history of the patient. When she finished going over the file, she looked at him and said, "Doesn't mean it's yours. She may have slept with other men, too."

"I don't think so, but it's possible. You need to test the baby's DNA against mine. Draw a blood sample. They should have the supplies in the lab."

"Okay. I'll be right back to get a sample from you," Jennifer said as she left.

Jennifer returned a few minutes later to draw his blood. "What are you going to do if it is a match?" she asked.

"I can't kill my own child for God's sake! And I won't let anyone else either."

"The baby may have some major birth defects from the German measles."

"I know, still I'm going to have to take my chances. If it does, I'll deal with them."

"What are you going to do?"

"I'm going to deliver it instead of aborting it."

"It may not be able to survive on its own at 28 weeks," Jennifer said, wanting him to understand the situation completely.

"I know. Are you with me on this?"

"They could take your license away. Are you sure you want to do this? We can't even run the test until she gets here."

"Yes. I know."

"Then, I'm with you."

"First, call St. Francis Hospital and let them know we may have a preemie for them to come and pick up. We will have her sign papers giving up her rights as a parent to me, the father. Also, she needs to sign a release form for the C-Section, if necessary. Don't let her read the first one, simply tell her the forms are both for the C-Section."

"Are you sure you don't want to talk to her first about this?" Jennifer asked.

"No. She chose to kill our baby. I don't want to talk to her or have anything to do with her. If I did and she refused, I could lose the baby. No."

"All right. I'll make the call. You find the forms you want signed," Jennifer said and left the room.

Kal sat down in the chair and ran his fingers through his hair. No matter what she'd been through, he couldn't agree with her decision to end their baby's life. What he was about to do was a huge risk. Nonetheless, what choice did he have? Either deliver the baby or kill it. Killing it wasn't even an option in his mind. This was his child and he would never be able to live with himself if he performed this abortion and murdered his own child. He took an oath to save lives and that was what he was going to do today. She didn't want this baby but he did. His mind was made up, he was delivering the baby. It couldn't be a coincidence he was here today at the clinic. God had wanted him here.

* * * *

It was finally here. The day she'd been waiting for. The week had gone slowly. One day she would cry for her unborn child, whereas the next she would be filled with anticipation to get on with her life and looked forward to feeling better. She fervently prayed God would forgive her for what she was about to do.

The drive was a short one. She walked into the waiting room and sat down after checking in at the desk. A couple of minutes later, a nurse escorted her back to a room to change out of her clothes. She put her clothes and purse away in a locker, as the nurse had instructed her and sat on the bed. Her heart was pounding in her chest. She was scared and nervous. The nurse came back in and handed her two forms to sign because they'd forgotten to get them signed at her last visit. They were release forms in case they needed to do a C-Section. Also, they would need to check the baby's blood type.

The nurse stuck a needle in her swollen belly for a few seconds, drawing out a small tube of blood for testing. Sensing Shana's agitated state, Jennifer reassured her abortions were quite routine nowadays and not to worry. She discussed with Shana how they would give her something for the pain through the IV she'd just put in her arm. For now, she had put something in the IV to help her relax. The nurse left and said she would be back to get her as soon as the doctor was ready.

Relax? Like that was even possible. Her pulse was racing. The impulse to flee was overpowering. Her mind kept focusing on the dead, lifeless body of her tiny baby. Maybe this was not such a good choice after all. Maybe she should simply get up, get dressed and go back home. Her eyes felt very heavy and her body was relaxing. It must be the drug the nurse put in the IV. Yes, she should get up and go home. Unfortunately, she couldn't keep her eyes open. Then before she could get up to leave and cancel the abortion, she was asleep.

* * * *

Jennifer finished running the DNA test and typing the baby's blood when Kal walked in. "It's a match," she said.

His palms were sweaty and his mind reeling. This was a life altering decision he was making. The baby was his and he would be responsible for this child going forward. Healthy or not. His life would be drastically changing and he prayed it would be for the best. In his mind, he was making the only available right decision regarding the baby.

"Okay. Let's do this. Ready?" Kal asked.

"Yes," Jennifer answered.

Kal walked out and headed to the surgery room.

Jennifer walked down the hall to Shana's room. Shana was fully relaxed and asleep. Good, she thought. She pushed the bed to the surgery room. Then she prepared for surgery. The St. Francis ambulance had just arrived and she brought the incubator to the back of the room.

Kal worked quickly to deliver the baby by C-Section. Jennifer made sure Shana was comfortable and still out and then assisted Kal. He had the baby out, a girl, and it looked fine, although he knew the complications would be on the inside, if any. The baby was a little over two pounds and breathing on her own. He handed Jennifer the baby to put in the incubator and clean her up. Then she would check the vitals of the baby.

Kal stitched up Shana. She was doing fine. He'd made the cut small knowing the baby would be small and it would make Shana's recovery quicker. He would have the clinic keep her overnight and possibly the next night, too.

"The vitals are good on the baby. What next?"

"She signed the papers, right? So I have custody."

"Yes."

"Have St. Francis take the baby to the hospital. It will be covered under my insurance. Good thing they don't know me over there. Simply tell them the father will be over there shortly."

"Okay," Jennifer said, as she left the room.

Kal stayed with Shana and the baby. He said silent prayers they would both be all right. The baby was doing well, so far. Which was good because it meant she was a fighter. He needed a tough little girl if he was going to be a single parent.

Jennifer came back in. "They'll be coming inside here in a couple of minutes. They are pulling up to the back door. I'll take Shana to the recovery room. One of Dr. Kessler's nurses, Kari, offered to stay the night with Shana. She said she could use the overtime hours."

"That's good. Just have her tell Shana she had to stay because we had to do a C-Section since the baby was too big and she wasn't able to

Taking Chances

have a normal, vaginal delivery. And we didn't want to take any chances with her life." He walked to the doors to hold them open while Jennifer pushed Shana out and to the recovery room.

"That's pretty much what I told her before I had her sign the papers," Jennifer said to Kal.

Jennifer was back in a few minutes. "I'll let the emergency team in and give them the paperwork. I can hear them knocking at the back door. Now, get out of here," she said, shooing him out of the room.

"I'll be in Dr. Kessler's office after I change out of these scrubs," Kal said, as he left the room.

A few minutes later, Jennifer walked into Dr. Kessler's office. "They left with the baby. Everyone from the clinic is gone except for Kari and she is with Shana."

"That's right. It is after 5:30," Kal said, looking at his watch. He picked up the copy of Shana's file he'd made for himself and stuffed it into his briefcase. "Let's get out of here."

They walked silently to their cars in the parking lot. "I'm going over to St. Francis to be with the baby," Kal said staring blankly toward the road.

"Mind if I stop over there tomorrow?" Jennifer asked.

"No, of course not. And... Thank you." Kal leaned over, hugged Jennifer for a moment and then released her.

"Kal, we are in the business of saving lives. That is exactly what we did today. And I do not regret it for one minute."

Kal's eyes were watering now. "You are the best nurse and friend anyone could ever have." With that, he got in his car and headed to St. Francis Hospital. He was going to see his daughter. Baby Paxton. Guess he would have to come up with a name. *God, please let her be okay.*

* * * *

Shana woke up to see a different nurse seated beside her bed. As soon as her eyes opened and she moved, the nurse stood up.

"How do you feel? It's all over and you're doing fine. They had to do a C-Section, because you weren't able to deliver normally. So you're spending the night here and I'll be staying with you," Kari said.

Shana was still a little out of it; however, she heard the word "over" and knew she'd killed her baby. What kind of person was she? "But I changed my mind," she mumbled and tears were falling wildly.

"Honey, oh I'm sorry. This is a normal reaction for women to change their minds after it's done. What you're feeling is perfectly normal. You must go over all the reasons you had for doing it and stay strong in your conviction that you made the right decision for yourself and your baby," Kari said, as she held Shana's hand.

"I was going to tell the nurse I changed my mind only I fell asleep."

"It will be okay. Don't dwell on it. It's over with."

"I suppose," Shana answered. The nurse was right. It was done and there wasn't anything she could do about it now.

"Let me get you something to drink. I'll be right back," Kari said.

"Yes, something to drink would be good."

Kari was good at her job. She'd spent many a night with a young woman who had chosen to abort her baby. At that point, it was done and all she could do was try to take the woman's mind off the abortion by talking about other things. It would be a tough night; nonetheless, she would see her patient through it. Besides, everything always looked brighter in the morning.

The morning came and Shana was all talked out and all cried out. She didn't have any friends so it was good for her to have Kari to talk to. Kari was sympathetic and offered good advice on moving forward with her life. The sun was shining bright and somehow her future seemed a little brighter. She asked God for his forgiveness for what she'd done and that he would help her move forward out of this massive state of depression she'd been in during her pregnancy. Yes, this was the first day of the rest of her life, or so the saying goes.

* * * *

The next day, Kal and Jennifer stood outside the window of the hospital nursery watching Baby Paxton. She'd beaten the odds and was free of defects. She was in the winning fifty percent.

"You need to make plans," Jennifer said.

"I know."

Taking Chances

"Your whole life is changed now. You'll need to buy all the baby stuff babies need and find a babysitter."

"I may have to leave Minnesota," Kal said, still staring at the baby behind the glass.

"Why?"

"My sister would love to have a baby to take care of, only she doesn't live in Minnesota. I'm not sure I should stay here anymore anyway. Especially after this."

"I understand. That makes sense. The baby will probably be in the hospital for a couple of weeks at least. Nevertheless you better start making plans right away."

"I will," Kal said as he looked at the baby again. Yesterday had been life changing. He was now a father because he took a chance and did what he believed was right. This was his daughter. The daughter he almost lost. That was what life was all about, taking chances.

Chapter Four

Two Years Later

    Shana parked her car and got out slowly, savoring the view, and the beautiful colors of autumn. The red Maples were just peaking along with the rich gold Aspens and Oaks. The air was warm due to a few lucky days of Indian Summer. She certainly did like this time of year. It was just that it was way too short and she really disliked what came after it. Winter. Yes, snowflakes could be very pretty especially during an early snow flurry, and the lawns looked ever so pristine covered in white. However, the beauty wore off quickly. Reality set in. The cold—bitter cold, made you feel like you would never be warm again. The slippery, icy roads that made you grip the wheel of the car with a death grip. Yes, you literally held on to it for dear life. Only the slightest patch of ice could send the car into the ditch or into another car. It absolutely felt like you were risking your life to go to work, or anywhere for that matter.

    Well enough of that, it was a beautiful day and she would be gone before the snow fell. She walked slowly, as if savoring every minute, into Champps Americana, a local bar and restaurant. She was meeting her friends, all four of them—three were co-workers and the fourth was her therapist, Tara. They'd insisted she have a proper going away party.

    Tara, a woman in her forties with short brown hair approached and embraced Shana. "It's so good to see you, Shana."

    "I'm glad you could make it," Shana said.

    "You look great! I so envy you, getting out of Minnesota!" Tara said.

Taking Chances

"Thanks, I'm looking forward to missing the first snow," Shana answered and turned towards the hostess.

"The rest of your party is here, so if you'll follow me," the hostess said and escorted them into the dining area. Shana and Tara followed.

Casey, Diane and Nancy all got up from their chairs to greet her with a hug.

"Tara, these are my friends, Casey, Diane and Nancy," Shana said as each one got up and shook Tara's hand. "And this is Tara, my therapist and now close friend."

Bless their hearts! They'd decorated her chair with balloons—not just ordinary balloons, palm tree balloons. On the table sat a very delicious looking palm tree cake, covered with chocolate and coconut. "You guys shouldn't have," she said as the tears welled in her eyes. No one had ever done this for her before.

"But you deserve it," Diane said as all three of them hugged her at the same time.

Everyone was seated at the table finally. "Where did you get a palm tree cake?" Shana asked.

"I made it," Casey said. "I hope you like it."

"It's awesome!" Shana replied.

They all ordered from the menu and chattered about shared events they'd attended. Casey, Diane and Nancy all worked part time at Starbucks with her. Starbucks was her first job after being let go from Ultimate Promotions. She'd been there a year.

She'd met Tara almost two years ago. It seemed so long ago. Almost like a lifetime ago. She'd been so depressed she'd come close to giving up on life all together. Thank God, she'd met Tara. A week after the abortion, she went to the free clinic for a checkup. Everything was fine except for the fact she was even more depressed after the abortion, if that was even possible. Only now, they could give her some meds to take for it. At that point, she was willing to try almost anything if it would make her feel good. Make her feel alive again. She started taking the pills right away and by the time her first appointment with Tara came, she was already feeling so much better. Tara was the therapist/counselor the clinic had sent her to. Mainly they talked about everything that had happened to her recently. Which were all her losses. Both parents, a child, a job and insurance.

Tara helped her to get through it all. She was off the meds now and feeling one hundred percent better. The part time job at Starbucks had helped immensely also. It gave her a place to go. She'd badly needed the social interactions it provided. And best of all Casey, Diane and Nancy came with the job. The three of them had quickly and easily accepted her as a friend. They were all single and dragged her out of her apartment, her safe place, to movies, shows and events. It gave her so much to look forward to. Even though Tara had not met them before, she knew all about them from Shana's counseling sessions.

"Open your gifts, Shana!" Nancy said, as she began handing her a package.

Shana opened the first one—a gift card for Starbucks and a book about things to see and do in Arizona. "Thanks, this will come in handy," she said holding the book up for them to see. "And you guys know how much I like Starbucks."

The next one was a Minnesota tote bag from the Mall Of America and a Starbucks gift card from Diane. "Thank you," she said holding the bag and card up for them to see.

"Don't want you to forget about Minnesota," Diane said. "Or Starbucks."

"Never," Shana laughed.

The third one was a Desperate Housewives T-shirt and a Starbucks gift card. "I love it. Thanks, Nancy." It was their favorite show. They'd spent hours and hours discussing each episode at work. Like what a hunk, Mike, the plumber was.

The last bag was from Tara. There were two books in it both titled *Starting Over*. One was a new self-help book on how to start over after suffering tragic losses and the other was a romance novel about a woman starting over after suffering huge losses in her life. The back cover blurb could've been about her life. How ironic. "Thanks, Tara."

Tara laughed. "At least you know the romance novel has a guaranteed happy ending! And I'm hoping yours will be too."

Taking Chances

The food came and they ate, while they continued to talk and laugh about their lives. It was getting late as they headed to their cars. Each one hugged her and wished her luck on her new venture.

"If it doesn't work out, you know we will be here and you can always come back," Casey said.

"Thanks, guys. You're the best friends I've ever had!" Shana said.

"You have all our numbers, so call us," Diane said.

"Call often," Tara said.

"I will," Shana said and got into her car before she started crying. She loved those four women. However she needed to move on and the new job waiting in Phoenix was perfect for her, and the climate there was exactly what she needed.

The next two days flew by as she packed all her meager belongings into boxes. The moving truck came on Friday morning to load her up. It was amazing to see how quickly they could load her boxes into the truck when it had taken her days and days to pack them. One hour was all it took.

Well, that was done, she thought, as the truck pulled onto the street and left. She would meet them at her new apartment in three days. She walked back into the apartment building and into her almost empty apartment. All that was left was a blow up bed to sleep on tonight, her suitcase, bathroom necessities and a clock/radio so she would wake up in the morning. After pumping up the bed and putting the sheets and blanket on it, she headed out for a drive. One thing left to do before leaving tomorrow morning and she wanted to do it before dark.

Her heart sank as she drove. Her parents. She was leaving them here in Minnesota and she was moving on to a new chapter in her life. Hopefully a much better, well happier one anyway. She had to say good-bye to them and the place to do that was at the cemetery. They weren't actually there anymore. She knew that. Nevertheless, that's where their bodies were buried and so that's where she would say good-bye to them.

Shana pulled into the Fort Snelling Cemetery and drove down the road to their gravesites. This cemetery was so large it was amazing anyone could find the gravesites they were looking for. Rows and rows of white headstones in perfectly aligned rows. It was peaceful here.

She'd give them that. Except, of course, for the airplanes flying overhead. But what could you expect when the cemetery was located between two airports.

She found the row she was looking for and pulled over. Shana reached for the silk flowers she'd bought to put on the grave and got out. When she reached the grave, she laid the flowers near the headstone.

"Mom, I just wanted to say goodbye. I'm leaving tomorrow to make a new start in a new warm city—Phoenix. I know we always talked about you moving there only you never got the chance. So, I'm going now while I still have the chance. I have a job again. A real job. I'm starting over. Alone. All by myself." Shana sat down on the grass beside the grave. "I miss you, Mom. I miss talking to you. I miss you too, Dad. I'll miss Minnesota, especially in the summer. I have to go now. I have a long drive tomorrow. Alone. Sometimes, I still feel so very alone, but I'm doing much better." Tears were falling down her cheeks and she wiped them away as she stood up.

"I suppose this is really rather silly. Here I am, a grown woman standing in a cemetery talking to my dead parents. I do know you aren't actually here, you're in heaven. Somehow, I hope you can hear me. I have to go. I'll try to come back to visit, when I get back to Minneapolis."

Shana ran to the car, madly wiping her tear-streaked face. By the time she reached the car and got in, she was sobbing uncontrollably. After she was all cried out, she headed home. She really wasn't hungry even though she hadn't eaten all day so she swung through the Wendy's drive thru to get some food. She ate it in the car as her mind madly filed through memories of her parents.

It had been a long day but finally she was in her apartment ready to go to sleep on her blow up bed. She was emotionally drained and sleep came quickly. Morning arrived even sooner, and before she knew it, she was on the freeway headed south. The temperature had dropped to 45 degrees overnight, so it made leaving even easier.

Six hours later, she pulled into Kansas City. She stopped for gas and food and continued on. Finally, after another six hours of driving down the lonely freeway, she pulled into Oklahoma City. She found a

Taking Chances

Holiday Express hotel with a Sonic Drive-In next door. Once she checked in, she walked over to the drive-in to get a burger, fries and a sundae. Even though it was nine in the evening, the temperature was still around 75 degrees. She knew she was going to like the warm temperatures of Phoenix. She headed back to her room. Morning would come quickly and she still had a long drive ahead.

It had been tough to get up in the morning. She was tired; nonetheless, she got up knowing if she didn't, she wouldn't make Phoenix before dark. Now, six hours later she pulled into Albuquerque. She filled her tank, grabbed a sandwich and was back on the road again within thirty minutes.

About nine she pulled into Phoenix and her apartment complex. She opened the door to her apartment and carried in her blow-up bed and bags. It didn't take long before she had the bed ready and herself ready to go to sleep. The truck would be here early in the morning and she wanted to be awake.

The truck arrived promptly at nine, the next morning. Within three hours, they had everything unloaded and were gone. Shana spent the rest of the day unpacking. By evening, she felt like she was organized and somewhat comfortable in her new home. She set out pictures of her parents and sat down on the couch to view her results.

The room looked well put together and homey. It looked and felt comfortable. All she needed now was some groceries, but it was late, so she would wait until morning. Heck, there was always a Domino's Pizza. She could have it delivered. It was Saturday night, she had a television and soon she would have pizza!

Sunday was her day to check out the city in which she now lived. She found a grocery store and bought groceries. She drove past the hospital where she would start her new job tomorrow. This job was her new start in life. She was excited to be a part of the real world again with a full time job and benefits. With insurance. Yes, she would have insurance again. Vacation, sick days and even a 401K. Yes, she truly was a real person again. She even got to do something she liked, and was good at. She was the new Events Planner for the Arizona Memorial Hospital in Scottsdale. She would be in charge of their information booths at trade shows for Job Fairs and would also set up all hospital and employee events.

Before she knew it, it was Monday morning and she was on her way to the hospital. Her first stop was Human Resources. After filling out numerous forms, she was given a tour of the hospital and escorted to her new office.

Shana sat down at her desk and looked out the window. There was a smile on her face. This definitely was the first day of the rest of her life and she was going to make the best of it. It had been a long time coming; finally she was feeling happy again. Really happy.

* * * *

Thursday was the yearly Medical Job Fair at the Phoenix Convention Center. Shana spent her entire first three months at Arizona Memorial Hospital preparing for this big day. The hospital recruited and hired the majority of their nurses, doctors and administrative employees at this event. Anyone graduating in the medical fields, hoping to land their first job attended. She was responsible for all the advertising/marketing literature to be distributed, all the signage for the booth, and scheduling slots to keep the booth manned with hospital personnel.

People from various positions in the hospital would be there to answer questions from potential new employees and to accept resumes. Mostly nurses and administrative people worked the booth. Rarely did doctors show up. If they were there, it was only to give mini seminars or to attend one of the mini seminars presented by other doctors. Shana would be there to be sure everything went smoothly and to make sure the booth was manned at all times.

She was nervous. This was her first show for her new job and she wanted everything to go well. The hospital had sent her to a couple of one-week conferences on job fairs and events planning strategies. She'd also flown to Chicago and Dallas to attend their Medical Job Fairs. She was nervous but felt good about the event. She was prepared and everything was ready to go.

Shana left work early to grab dinner and head home. She wanted to get to bed early because she needed to be at the Convention Center

Taking Chances

bright and early. She spent the day, today, setting up the booth. She was drained. Tomorrow was her big day and she would enjoy it. Her fingers were crossed hoping everything would go as she had planned.

* * * *

Arizona Memorial Hospital's booth looked sharp, very eye pleasing as she approached it. The backdrop was filled with pictures of the hospital, the different specialty floors, doctors, nurses and administrative staff of the hospital.

The main doors to the halls would open in five minutes and she'd been informed the future graduates from the colleges and universities were already lined up and waiting to get in. Two nurses were ready to answer questions and two people from the administrative staff were available to hand out literature and take applications or resumes.

There was a loud banging noise as the doors swung open and were latched to keep them open. People flooded the aisles. Shana grabbed a handful of brochures to help hand out. As an extra enticement to turn in an application, they had canvas bags with the hospital name embroidered on them to give out when a job seeker submitted a resume.

It was after one, when Shana headed out to grab a sandwich for lunch from one of the food vendors. As she walked to a table to sit down she glanced down the hall filled with people, then froze. She reached for a chair to steady herself and quickly set the food tray down on the table, before sitting down, trembling.

Chapter Five

There simply wasn't anyway it could be him. She was in Arizona not Minnesota. It couldn't be him, although it sure had looked like him. Why would he be here? She had to get a grip. She'd only seen a glimpse of the man. It couldn't be him. She hadn't seen him for almost three years, so what were the odds she'd run into him now? And in a totally different state, besides. No, it couldn't have been him. And even if it was, so what? He probably wouldn't even remember her. Or recognize her. Her hair was layered and she was dressed much more sophisticated then when he met her. Hell, she was only a one-night stand to him. So he wouldn't remember or recognize her. She had nothing to worry about.

Shana glanced down the hall again. There was no sign of the man she'd seen a few minutes earlier. She picked up her sandwich and shook off the odd feeling she'd had when she saw that man. Her thoughts drifted off for a moment to her lost baby. A place she didn't want to go. She quickly redirected her thoughts to the job fair.

As Shana walked back to the booth, she couldn't help scanning the crowd for the man who looked like Kal. There was no one who looked like him. She felt better by the time she got back to the booth. The crowd had thinned somewhat nevertheless was still steady. Throughout the day, she scanned the crowd. She'd managed to convince herself the man she saw only looked similar to Kal, but wasn't him.

The rest of the day was pretty much uneventful. The booth equipment was all packed up. Her first event was done and now behind her. It had gone extremely well and she felt proud. It was a huge accomplishment for her new career and herself. She'd come a long way and, best of all, she really liked her new job. It was fun and exciting. Yet, it was challenging and she liked that.

Driving home, she thought about Kal. She couldn't stop thinking about him. What if that man actually was him? What if he had moved to Arizona, too? What would she say to him if she ever saw him again? Well, it just couldn't be him and she would never see him again so she simply didn't need to waste any more time thinking about it. And that was that and she wasn't going to think about it or him anymore.

* * * *

"Nice job, Shana," her boss, Carol said.

"Thank you," Shana replied.

"We had a record number of resumes turned in yesterday."

"That's great. I know we were extremely busy."

"Have to run to a meeting, catch you later," Carol said looking at her watch, as she headed out the door.

Shana sat down at her desk and breathed a sigh of relief. Whew! She'd done it. Her first event and her boss was pleased. Now on to the next project. She had various luncheons and Christmas parties to plan. There were appointments at local restaurants to check out their banquet facilities and taste their food. First, she needed to go to a meeting with the nurse supervisors to see what they suggested for their Christmas party. The meeting was on the sixth floor.

Standing in the elevator waiting for the door to close, a doctor walked up the hallway and Shana gasped and grabbed the railing in the elevator just as the door closed. It was him—Kal.

The elevator stopped at the next floor, the door opened and Shana stepped out. She proceeded directly into the restroom, into a stall and closed the door. Her hands were shaking. She wasn't sure why. She assumed he was a doctor at Arizona Memorial Hospital, which meant sooner or later she would run into him. She also knew, eventually, she would have to talk to him. What would she say? *I didn't know where to find you and our baby is dead?* But then, he would have no way of knowing what had happened or what she'd done, so she wouldn't have to say anything. Heck, she didn't even have to acknowledge she knew him. It would be up to him. If he didn't say anything, she wouldn't either. She would avoid him at all costs. She regained her composure and went to her meeting.

After the meeting, she pulled up the directory of doctors at Arizona Memorial Hospital on the computer. She scanned through the list. There was only one doctor with the name of Kal. Kalvin Paxton, General Practitioner. Now that she knew he worked at Arizona Memorial Hospital, she would be sure to avoid him. After all, it was a big hospital, so it might be possible.

As the weeks passed, Shana checked all her meetings to see who would be attending. So far so good. She felt like she constantly had her guard up while in the halls. Watching for him. She'd been lucky, so far.

Today, her luck ran out. At lunchtime, she was in the cafeteria eating when Kal walked in. He didn't look her way, however she had seen him. She didn't think he'd seen her. He went through the line, got his lunch and sat at a table outside on the patio. She'd gotten a good look at him on his way to the patio. The windows had a reflective coating on the outside, so you couldn't see in from the outside even though you could see out from the inside. This allowed her to observe him fully without him knowing.

She'd forgotten how handsome he was. In the bright sunlight even, he was hot! No wonder she'd been attracted to him. She was sure all the single nurses in this hospital must be after him. Granted that he was still single. That was something she hadn't thought of. Maybe he'd gotten married. It had been almost three years. He certainly could have. She would have to check that out without being too apparent in her motive. And what was her motive? Well, if he were married maybe he wouldn't acknowledge her even if he recognized her. That would be great.

But man-o-man he was good looking. Tall, dark hair, nice body. He must work out every day. If he was single and they hadn't had that past encounter, she would actually be interested in dating him. Although they did have a past, and he would never understand why she did what she had to do. Her heart was racing just looking at him. It was a good thing he couldn't see through the glass to see her blatantly assessing him.

Taking Chances

The past was the past. There wasn't anything that could be done to change what had happened. So maybe it would only be her secret and he would never have to know? A part of her wanted that to be true, but she knew and she would eventually have to tell him. However, only if they went out. So she would have to make sure that never happened.

Chapter Six

Kal couldn't believe his eyes as he carried his tray to a table on the cafeteria patio. Shana. It was her! What was she doing here? His palms were sweating and his forehead perspiring profusely. After moving to Phoenix, he'd convinced himself he would never see her again. She could potentially ruin his career, his life. Maybe it was only someone who looked like her. After all, he was in Phoenix and she was in Minnesota. At least that was where she was supposed to be. Where he'd left her. Unfortunately, many Minnesotans came to Phoenix to vacation or visit friends or relatives. Maybe she was just visiting someone in the hospital and would be going back to Minnesota soon. He would simply have to be careful not to run into her while she was here. But then again, they claim everyone has a twin, so maybe this woman he'd just seen looked like her. Yes! That had to be it. In fact, this woman looked different. The hair was different and she was dressed very professional yet still sexy. He was attracted to her. Damn!

As he pulled into the hospital parking lot the next morning, he wondered if she was in the hospital now. He reached for a napkin lying on the passenger seat and wiped his perspiring forehead. "Get a grip!" he shouted out loud.

He got out of the car and walked into the hospital using the doctor's entrance. Kal got to his office and sunk into his desk chair. There just wasn't any point getting all worked up about this. Odds were it wasn't her so he was going to forget about it. Hell, he should've never come in today. He wasn't even supposed to be here. He'd taken the day off to go golfing with a friend; unfortunately, his friend had to go out of town unexpectedly and canceled. So he decided to come in and do some paperwork and attend the doctor/vendor luncheon today. He would attend it since he was here and then he was leaving. For now, he was going to not think about her anymore. At least not this morning. He had paperwork to do and that would take his mind off her.

* * * *

Shana's day had started out great nevertheless wasn't going as smoothly as planned. The vendors giving the doctors' luncheon had experienced flight delays and requested to reschedule for tomorrow. This all sounds simple in theory although trying to reschedule doctors wasn't so easy with their tight schedules. She had to and would need to see how many could attend tomorrow. The incentive for the doctors to attend was the vendors always sprang for a top quality luncheon with great food and expensive complimentary gifts. This was why the doctors cleared their schedules to attend. Granted, the doctors always wanted to be informed of any new drugs and equipment, too.

Shana called the caterer to reschedule and sent out an email to the doctors who had confirmed their attendance and to all who had declined. Hopefully, the numbers would come out the same because some who accepted wouldn't be able to make it now, then again some who declined would be able to come. They had to reply by noon, so they'd have a count for the caterers. Shana's assistant was in charge of getting the new counts and printing a list.

It was lunchtime and the counts had come in only slightly over the original, so they would be fine. Thankfully, the room she'd reserved for the luncheon wasn't being used for anything else, so they could leave the decorations up for tomorrow.

Shana walked into the luncheon room to inform the janitor to leave up the decorations since the event had been rescheduled for tomorrow. She turned and walked toward the door to the hallway, the janitor apparently left open, to see if Meg was there yet. She stopped abruptly in the doorway. Meg was a few feet away talking to a doctor. That doctor was Kal. Meg's back was to the door so she couldn't see Shana. But Kal faced Shana and looked directly at her. Shana stared at him. She was sure she looked as white as a ghost, because she felt all the blood drain from her face. She could hear Meg still talking, but Kal was staring right at her. In that moment she knew it was him. He said nothing only nodded to Meg, turned around and walked away.

Shana turned slowly and looked for a chair. She felt faint and needed to sit down. As soon as she reached the chair at the closest table, she sat down and rested her head in her hands with her elbows braced on her knees. She took deep breaths of air. She needed to relax and calm down.

"Shana, are you okay?" Meg asked.

"Dizzy," Shana managed.

"Do you want me to get a doctor?"

"No, I'll be fine." Shana forced herself to sit up.

"Are you sure? You don't look so good."

"Yes, I just got a little dizzy for a moment," Shana said and stood up.

"Maybe you should go home. You look pale. We don't have anything else today since the luncheon was rescheduled. I can take care of the counts and any late emails we get," Meg suggested.

"Actually, I think I will." Shana rose from the chair and walked to the elevator.

Shana collected her purse and bag, closed up her office and walked to her car. Every minute she prayed she wouldn't run into him. When she made it, she opened the car door and sank down in the seat. "Thank heavens." She started the car and drove out of the parking lot. She didn't want to go home so she drove to the mall and pulled up at Starbucks. She ordered a sandwich and frozen coffee drink. She needed to think. She walked outside to the patio tables, sat down and ate her sandwich. Maybe eating would help since she hadn't eaten anything yet today.

The Starbucks was part of an outside strip mall surrounding the main, larger indoor mall. It was located on the end of one of the buildings and the outside patio had a rock water fountain and garden filled with small cactus and azaleas. It certainly was decorated quite ornately and helped her to relax.

She had to figure out what she was going to do. Now, that she was certain it was him. He had stared deeply into her eyes, as if he was trying to see inside her. The recognition was definitely there. He recognized her yet he hadn't said a word, just left. Why? Was he embarrassed because he left her apartment that morning and never contacted her again? Maybe he simply didn't want to acknowledge her because he thought she was the type of woman who took men home all the time and had no morals. That was probably it. He thought she was a whore. And he was a prestigious doctor. Actually, that would be fine with her. They could behave as if they'd never met before—be socially polite at work and only talk to each other if absolutely necessary at the hospital. That could work. Yes, everything would be okay.

Shana spent the rest of the day shopping and relaxing. Shopping always used to make her feel good so it was worth a try. She decided to treat herself to a new suit for the luncheon tomorrow. She wanted to look her best, if she was going to spend the afternoon tomorrow being observed by Kal. Why she cared though, she wasn't sure.

* * * *

After leaving Shana standing in the doorway of the luncheon room, Kal literally ran down the stairs. He was breathing heavily as he opened the door to the second floor, then forced himself to walk slowly down the hall to his office. Once in his office he changed back into jeans and sat down at his desk. He turned on his computer and found the hospital's employee listing. He scrolled down to the marketing department and found the title Events Planner and there was her name, Shana Madden.

"Damn!" Kal swore. He put his head in his hands with his elbows braced on the desk. "Shit!" What was he going to do? Well, first, he would call it a day. He wasn't supposed to be here, anyway. He only came for the luncheon. The one of which Shana was in charge.

"Hell, I'm out of here," he said as he got up from the chair, grabbed his keys and left. He didn't know where he was going except he wanted to get out of there before he ran into her again. He needed a plan of some sort. He got in his Corvette and just drove, until he pulled into a shopping mall and eyed the Starbucks. He should get a coffee, sit down and try to relax so he could think this through. Though, as he parked, he knew coffee just wasn't going to cut it. No, he needed a drink. Yes, a glass of wine would work. That would relax him. So instead of Starbucks, he walked into the Macaroni Grill, got a patio table and sat down. After smelling the delicious aromas from the kitchen, Kal ordered a pasta entrée to go with his wine. He looked out at the beautiful waterfall and garden separating the Macaroni Grill from Starbucks on the end of the next building.

Kal recalled the unfortunate event at the hospital. He must accept the fact they now both worked at the same hospital. *What was he going to do?* He couldn't make her leave, and he didn't exactly want to leave either. He liked Arizona Memorial Hospital. It was a good place to work and he liked the people there. Nonetheless, they would continue to run into each other and he certainly didn't want to see her again. Hell, he hadn't wanted to see her EVER! And that had worked out great.

He hated her for what she'd tried to do to their baby. No one should do that to an innocent baby. He'd read the files and knew she had a somewhat logical reason for wanting to abort the baby. But my God, it was his daughter. Beautiful Kalsha. Every day he thanked God for placing him at the clinic on that fateful day so he could save her life. Jennifer, his nurse, told him the nurse who took care of Shana on that life-altering night said Shana woke up crying and pleading to stop the abortion because she'd changed her mind. Only it had been too late—the abortion was done. At the time, he really hadn't given a second thought to that revelation. Seeing her today and knowing about her change of heart, he knew there was a chance, although slight, he might be able to forgive her. After all, if it weren't for Shana, he wouldn't have his daughter. Unfortunately, that was something Shana would never find out, because he would never tell her. He would simply have to treat her as an acquaintance and act like nothing had happened between them.

Against his better judgment, he recalled her free flowing blond hair, her sexy figure, and her lush lips. Lips that begged to be kissed. He remembered touching every luscious curve of her body before joining his body with hers. Hell, he'd tried so hard to forget that night. To forget her. To forget what she'd tried to do, only he couldn't. Every time he looked at his daughter, he saw Shana's face, no matter how hard he tried not to. A part of him hated her. The other part knew he

Taking Chances

could've fallen in love with her. If only he'd been able to find her after their night of raw passionate sex. Yes, that was what it really was. It had been raw, fast and hard. But, oh so good! He'd waited too long to have sex and he'd guess it'd been a while for her, too. The physical attraction and chemistry was strong that night and obviously, it was still strong today.

Kal finished his wine and set the glass down. The situation was a Hell of a mess. One minute he wanted to pick up where they left off, and the next he wanted to literally wring her neck for what she'd done. Well, almost done. Unfortunately, there was no going back. What he'd done wasn't really right, either. He should've talked to her and maybe they could have worked something out. Maybe if he'd let her know she wasn't alone in the situation and that he could help. Maybe then, he wouldn't have had to take their baby away from her. Now was not the time for maybes. It was over and done. They both had to live with the choices they'd made. There was no going back. All he could do was avoid her from now on and hope she would choose to do the same. There was no future for them.

Kal paid his tab and walked through the main part of the restaurant to the doors leading to the parking lot. As he stepped out, he saw a woman with long blonde hair walking down the parking lot row to her car. When she got to her car, she stopped and turned her face his way to let the wind blow the misplaced strands of hair from her face. For a moment, he saw her face. He was mesmerized. He stared at her. She opened the car door and bent to get in, baring one leg as she pulled her skirt up slightly. He lifted his eyes from her smooth, tanned calf and thigh to her face. Yes, it was Shana. "What the Hell!" He just couldn't get away from her. The leg shot got a definite response from his body. "Hell!" This was going to be tough. However, he had no choice; he had to do everything possible to avoid her.

Kal stepped out of the restaurant and let the door close behind him. Shana's car turned onto the main parking lot lane, which was in front of him. She turned her head his way to look for cars and looked right at him. She regrouped quickly and finished the turn. She'd seen him—he knew it. He couldn't get away from her.

* * * *

Shana managed to leave the mall's parking lot. But how she wasn't sure. What was he doing? Was he following her? That was just plain too absurd. Could he possibly have left after their encounter at the hospital, too? This was entirely all too weird that they ended up in the same city even, much less working at the same hospital. And now at the same mall. Odds were it wouldn't happen again—his showing up at the mall, although it would at the hospital. She could deal with it as long as there were other people around, and if they weren't alone it would be okay. She would simply have to be sure she was never alone with him.

God, he looked good standing there in jeans and a golf shirt with the wind blowing his hair. She would not remember their night together. It was so long ago. Yet her body was traitorous and she felt her pulse quicken at the thought. It was over three years ago, and that was the problem right there. It had been too long with no sex. *Maybe she needed a man.* However, it sure wasn't going to be Kal. He was the last person with whom she'd have sex. How ironic was that? He *was* the last person with whom she'd had sex.

* * * *

Shana woke up the next morning feeling tired, having tossed and turned most of the night. The hospital today was the last place she wanted to go. Then again, since she liked her job and needed her job, she got up and went through her morning routine. The new, sexy, form fitting black power pantsuit hanging on her bathroom door beckoned her. She took extra care with her make-up and hair this morning. She wanted to look her best, not that it should matter. The reflection in the mirror portrayed a classy, sexy, professional businesswoman. She looked good. If nothing else, she would let Kal know he'd passed up a very hot lady.

She managed to get to the hospital without running into Kal.

"Wow! You look great," Meg said as Shana entered her office.

"Thanks," Shana answered.

"New suit?"

"Yes."

"Well, it definitely fits you perfectly."

"Do you think so? I wasn't sure if it was too—"

Taking Chances

"Sexy?" Meg offered.

"Yes."

"It's sexy, yet professional. You're certainly going to turn some heads at the luncheon today."

Shana thought that wasn't really her plan. She only wanted Kal to know what he'd passed up.

"Is there someone whose attention you're trying to catch?"

"No! Of course not. Simply wanted to look my best. So what's our count for the luncheon?"

"Here's the list of attendees. I just printed it."

Shana took the list to her desk. Sitting down, she scanned the list of names quickly not realizing she was so tense her breathing wasn't normal. There it was. Kalvin Paxton. He would be there. She sat back in the chair releasing her breath with a sigh. What had she been hoping? That his name wouldn't be on the list? Of course it would. Why would he not come? He certainly wouldn't be afraid to see her, would he? No, of course not. She was the one who was stressed about being in the same room with him.

Meg appeared in the doorway. "Shana, I'm going to head down to the luncheon room and make sure everything is ready."

Shana looked up. "Good, you go ahead, I'll meet you down there in about an hour. I'm going to finish up some other business first."

"Okay, I'll call you if there are any problems—although there shouldn't be," Meg said as she walked out.

Shana walked over to the window and stared out towards the pond of water with its fountain shooting water upwards from the center. It was beautiful surrounded by perfectly manicured lawns and gardens with rich colors of red and yellows—Tulips and Daffodils. She would've preferred to be outside walking on the path surrounding the pond. Some people here actually thought of it as a small lake however coming from Minnesota, the land of 10,000 lakes, one knew what real lakes looked like. Yet on the other hand, being that Phoenix was a desert, the pond was a refreshing sight that brought back memories of Minnesota and its lakes, in the summer that is. It was cold there now and soon the lakes would freeze. Yes, the pond was a welcome sight that beckoned her. Just watching the movement of the water through the window was relaxing. Shana forced herself to take some deep refreshing breaths, and she felt her body relax.

"Back to work," she said, sat down at her computer and began tackling her emails.

There was an email from Tara, her therapist from back home, checking to see how the new job was going, asking if she liked Phoenix. And letting her know it was twenty-five degrees and snowing lightly in Minnesota.

She would send Tara an email this afternoon. It would be good to tell her about Kal. Tara was the only one who knew her whole story and would understand what she was going through. Simply knowing she could express her feelings about seeing Kal again to Tara made her feel better and decreased her stress level.

Shana finished checking and answering her emails and checked her voice mail for messages. There were only a couple voice messages so she made the return calls, knowing they wouldn't take much time.

Naturally, the phone rang right when she was about to leave. It was the Scottsdale Desert Oasis Golf Course's clubhouse event coordinator calling to confirm the golf event the hospital had planned for next week. This was a call she needed to take. It ended up being a long call, however she still had plenty of time. It was about eleven when she finally got on the elevator. Everything should be ready to go since Meg hadn't called with any problems.

The elevator door opened and she caught herself checking the halls for any sign of Kal. No Kal. She didn't even know why she was looking for him when the luncheon wasn't for another hour or so. She really needed to relax and stop thinking about him. There wasn't even any reason to think she would be personally introduced to him. There wasn't anything to worry about. She would just do her job and try not to be in the same part of the room he was in. After all, it was a big room.

The hour went fast and soon the doctors were arriving to check in. Thankfully, Meg was checking them in and handing out the nametags.

Shana went back into the luncheon room to check with the vendors to be sure there wasn't anything else they needed. She and Meg had already placed the goodie bags on all the chairs. The Medtronic

Taking Chances

vendors had a power point presentation and short video to show. After lunch was served, they would give out the prizes. The prizes were amazing and expensive. Ronald Palmer golf clubs, a laptop computer, a new LCD flat screen TV, the latest IPAD and a trip to Las Vegas staying at the Bellagio. It was no wonder the doctors made a point of showing up at these luncheon events.

Shana glanced out the door toward the check in table where Meg sat. The line was long, so she went out to help her. She began checking off names while Meg handed out the nametags. She was so busy looking for the names that when she looked up finally to see how long the line was, she saw Kal across the table from her. She stared at him and couldn't make her lips move to speak. "Kalvin Paxton," he said staring back at her.

Meg reached towards Kal, handing him his nametag, only he didn't even look her way simply continued staring at Shana. "Your name tag, Dr. Paxton," she said looking from Kal to Shana.

"Thank you," Kal finally said, looking at Meg and taking his nametag from her extended hand. He turned back to look at Shana, who felt shock setting in. He nodded to her, then turned and entered the room.

"Shana, everything okay?" Meg asked.

"Yes ... Yes it is." Shana helped Meg finish up with the few doctors left in line. What she truly wanted to do was leave. Every fiber in her body wanted to leave. The instinct to flee was overwhelming. Only she knew she couldn't. The only place she could go was into the luncheon room. Unfortunately, he was in there. Leaving wouldn't do her any good anyway. This was her job. She had to do this luncheon, regardless of her feelings. What she had to do was forget he was even there and do her job.

After everyone was checked in, they gathered up their files. Shana stood up. She knew Meg was going to say something about what happened earlier with Kal, however she thought Meg would wait until later. She was wrong.

"I take it you thought Dr. Paxton was hot?" Meg questioned.

"Dr. Paxton?" Shana managed to get out. She hadn't thought this would be Meg's conclusion about what had happened.

"Yes."

"Why do you say that?"

"You were staring at him and not saying a word. That's why."

"Well, yes, of course. Anyone would notice how handsome he is." *What was she saying?* She just admitted she found him attractive!

"He's considered a prime catch around the hospital," Meg stated.

"You don't say?" Shana asked, knowing it was probably true.

"I heard he doesn't date much though," Meg offered.

"He's single then?" Shana couldn't believe she had asked that.

"Oh, yes!" Meg stated proudly.

"Well, he certainly isn't my type," Shana said, knowing she had to end this conversation right now.

"Right. Wouldn't have guessed that by the way you looked at him. No, let me reword that. The way you two looked at each other."

"Enough on that subject, we have work to do," Shana said as they both closed the doors to the room and made their way over to their table. Shana scanned the room as she sat down. *Where was he?* She needed to know. Why, she wasn't sure, but she needed to know. Because if she didn't know, she wouldn't be able to watch him to see if he was watching her.

"Just in case you're interested, Dr. Paxton is sitting two tables over and has been watching you every minute since we walked in."

"Damn!" Shana said as she turned to see where he was seated and looked right into his eyes. He nodded and she turned away. "Why is he doing that?"

"Maybe he likes what he sees?" Meg answered stating the obvious.

"Right," Shana said. He was probably remembering her in bed, but of course, she wouldn't say that aloud, although it was probably true.

Just then, servers placed salad bowls in front of them. Shana tried to concentrate on eating her salad. She had that odd feeling a person gets when someone is watching them. She knew he was still watching her, but finally shook it off and went to check with the vendors since it was about time to start the presentation. Everything was ready so she returned to her table to sit down. The lights were lowered for the presentation and video. At least then, she wouldn't be able to see him watching her and he wouldn't be able to see her.

Taking Chances

   Shana got caught up in the video. Medtronics certainly had some cutting edge new technology for the medical field. The lights went up. The video was over and the Medtronics vendors had allowed time for questions. The doctors asked intellectual medical questions which she didn't understand. Many answers were directed to the portfolio hand out that had been placed on the tables.
   Shana was dreading the next part of the luncheon, which was the prizes, mainly because she and Meg were to assist the vendors.
   They were almost done and so far, no one at Kal's table had won anything. There was one prize left and she would be handing out the prize. It was the grand prize, the Las Vegas trip. Her chest felt tight and she couldn't breathe. She knew she was holding her breath, still she couldn't stop. Finally, the name was announced. She let out her breath when it wasn't Kal's name. Unfortunately, the winner was seated at Kal's table.
   Shana walked to the table hoping she wouldn't trip since everyone, including Kal, was watching her. She made it to the table and handed the winner the envelope containing the travel information. She looked at the winner and smiled.
   "Congratulations," she said.
   "Thank you," he responded.
   Shana nodded and walked to her table, not giving Kal a glance even though she felt his eyes on her. The luncheon was finally over and the doctors were talking and mingling with each other on their way out.
   Shana and Meg talked to the caterers as they began to finish up clearing the tables. The communications department was busy disconnecting the video equipment. She was not going to look for him, however just as she turned around, she almost collided with Kal.
   "Shana, I wanted to introduce you to Dr. Paxton. He is going to be your liaison for the golf event next week," Dr. Tanner stated as he and Kal walked up.
   "Oh, I thought you were, Dr. Tanner," Shana countered, hoping there was some mistake.
   "I've decided to pass it on to some young blood. I've done it for the last ten years. It's time to hand it over and Dr. Paxton fits the bill," Dr. Tanner said smiling at Kal.

"Nice to meet you. I'm Dr. Paxton," Kal said extending his hand to her.

Shana looked at his hand and knew she had to shake it. She watched as her hand extended to meet his. Their hands touched. "Nice to meet you, Kal," Shana said as she felt her face flush. Her body burned as if it was on fire when her hand touched his.

"Shana, I look forward to working with you," he said still holding her hand.

"Shana, the janitor needs to talk to you," Meg said as she walked up to rescue Shana.

"Sorry. I have to go," Shana said, turned and walked away with Meg.

"We'll talk later," Kal said to Shana's retreating back.

Kal watched her walk away. The suit she wore snugly fit every curve of her body. Her hips swayed provocatively as she walked. Her fragrance lingered, stirring up memories even after she'd gone. He'd never felt such a strong attraction simply from touching a woman's hand. Her whole presence was sensual and alluring. He wanted to touch every inch of her body, not just shake her hand. He watched her talking to the janitor. She was smiling and laughing. God help him but he wanted her. Again.

"Have you two met before?" Dr. Tanner asked.

"What?" Kal asked as his visual memory of their first meeting was interrupted.

"When she called you Kal it sounded as if she knew you."

"It's on my nametag," Kal answered. He had not given it any thought when she had said his name.

"Oh yes, it is," Dr. Tanner said as they walked out and down the hall.

"Now, you're sure you don't want to be the golf liaison?" Kal probed hoping that maybe he could get Dr. Tanner to change his mind.

"I'm sure. That Shana is quite an attractive young woman. Who knows maybe you two will hit it off."

"Not looking, remember?" Kal reminded him.

"We'll see," Dr. Tanner stated and walked into his office. Kal continued down the hall to his own office.

Taking Chances

He'd completely forgotten Dr. Tanner mentioning the golf liaison thing earlier in the week. He hadn't agreed to do it then again he hadn't declined either. Now what was he going to do? The physical attraction between him and Shana was so strong. If he wasn't careful, the desires of his body would win and there was no telling what would happen next whether he planned it or not. Whether he wanted it to or not, may not be a deciding factor. And seeing her on a daily basis would only fuel the smoldering fire.

Chapter Seven

    Shana sat at her computer typing a long email to Tara explaining what had happened to her in Phoenix. She was entirely convinced she was the unluckiest person in the whole world. Simply look at all the things she'd had to deal with in the last couple of years. Most people don't have that many bad things happen to them their entire lives and if they do, they are spread out over an entire lifetime. Really, what were the odds she would ever run into Kal again much less end up working at the same place? Then for that place to be thousands of miles from home? Maybe she should never have left Minnesota. She ended the email and hit send.

    It was after five and Meg had already left. Shana got her bags together and turned off the computer. She was ready to turn off the lights when the phone rang. She walked back over to the phone on her desk and saw Kal's name on the caller ID. She didn't know if she should pick up the phone receiver or not. What did he want? Why was he calling her? Especially after five? It rang again. She wasn't sure how or why, nonetheless her hand reached for the phone and picked it up.

    "This is Shana," she said.

    "It's Kal. I'm glad I caught you before you left."

    "Why?" Shana asked, completely caught off guard.

    "We need to talk," Kal stated matter-of-factly.

    "Why?" Shana asked again.

    "I think it would be best if we talk before we work on this golf tournament together."

    "Talk?" she managed to get out.

Taking Chances

"Since we'll be working together at the hospital, it may be in both our best interests to talk first. How about meeting me after work tomorrow for a drink?" Kal asked.

"Oh-I'm not sure—" she barely got out.

"It won't hurt, I promise. Meet me at the Desert Rose at six tomorrow night," Kal offered.

"This is so awkward," Shana managed to finally answer.

"Agreed. So tomorrow night then?" he asked.

"Okay."

"Great! I'll put you down in my date book. See you then," Kal stated and ended the call.

Date book? Shana set the phone back down on the receiver while staring at the caller id as it went blank. Had he thought they were going on a date tomorrow? No. He couldn't possibly be thinking that. Could he? They were only meeting to talk. About what she wasn't exactly sure though.

God only knew there were things they needed to talk about. Unfortunately, there were things she couldn't talk about. Not with him. At least not yet, though she did have questions she wanted to ask him. Like why he never called her after their one-night stand together. And she really wanted to know why he'd left her the fifty-dollar bill. She wasn't so sure she could bring herself to ask that question, although she certainly did want to know what his answer would be.

Shana gathered up her purse and bag and headed out to her car. She walked outside to a beautiful clear sky and warm air. The weather in Phoenix was everything she'd thought it would be and she was glad to be here even if it meant having to deal with Kal. She would get through this. It was best to face him alone, away from the hospital, where no one else could witness or overhear their conversation. This was only between the two of them. The biggest obstacle she had to face was this strong attraction she felt towards Kal. An attraction that couldn't go anywhere. So they would simply meet, talk about their fateful evening and how it had ended without any further conversation, and then they would go their separate ways—doing their own jobs, being polite to each other socially and at work. Yes, that was how it was going to work and she wasn't going to give it another thought the rest of the evening.

Somehow, things never work out the way you plan. Tara read her email about Kal, and Shana's phone rang as soon as she walked into her apartment.

"Shana, it's Tara," came the voice on the other end of the phone.

"Tara! I sent you an email today before I left the hospital."

"I know. I just read it. Are you all right?" Tara asked.

"Yes, I'm fine."

"Good, I was worried after reading that Kal is there in Phoenix," Tara said.

"Shocking, isn't it? I still can't believe it. I mean what are the odds of this happening?" Shana asked.

"Extremely slim I'm sure."

"So are you sure he recognized you?" Tara asked.

"Yes."

"Did he say something to you?"

"Actually he called my office right after I sent your email."

"Why? What did he want?"

"He wants to meet for a drink after work tomorrow."

"Why?" Tara asked.

"He said we need to talk."

"How do you feel about that?"

"I suppose it's the best thing to do. To break the ice as they say."

"It can be good as long as you feel up to it," Tara offered.

"I have a few questions for him I'd like to have answered."

"Like?"

"Why he never called? Why he left the money?"

"Yes, you deserve answers," Tara said.

"Not sure I can bring myself to ask about the money though. It's so humiliating."

"Are you going to say anything about the pregnancy?" Tara asked.

"No, probably not ever."

"Okay. Are you sure you're up to this?"

"Yes," Shana answered with some hesitation.

"I'm sensing hesitation. Is there something else bothering you?"

Taking Chances

"Tara, he is so damn good looking. I'd forgotten. It's been close to three years since I last saw him."

"Are you attracted to him?"

"Yes! Isn't that crazy?"

"No, absolutely not. You had sex with the man, so you were obviously attracted to him then. So it's no wonder you're attracted to him now."

"That makes sense, although I know it can't go anywhere this time."

"Try to relax and don't stress out about it. You have some questions you need to have answered foremost. So focus on them for tomorrow."

"I will. It's so weird to spend the last couple years thinking about him and now having to see him almost daily."

"Yes, that will be tough. You're doing great though. You'll be fine. I'm so proud of you!" Tara said emphatically.

"Thanks, Tara."

"Call me tomorrow and let me know how it goes."

"Okay."

"Shana, you know you can call me anytime don't you?" Tara asked.

"Yes, but—"

"Shana, we are friends. Call me."

"Okay. I'll let you know what answers he gives to my questions. Talk to you tomorrow," Shana said as she hung up the phone.

* * * *

Kal drove home with Shana on his mind. He'd done it. He was finally going to talk to her. It'd been at least two years since he'd last seen her. Now he would have the opportunity to ask her some questions. Some he could ask and some he couldn't. But all in all, he needed to break the ice between them so they could work together. He needed to make sure she didn't know what he'd done. Because if she did, it was a whole new ballgame. He felt such a strong attraction to her though and he thought she'd felt it too. He could feel it when he shook her hand. He simply couldn't understand why she'd not looked for him when she'd gotten pregnant. Unfortunately, they couldn't have anything together now. It was just too late. Even if he wanted her, would he be able to forgive or forget what she tried to do. If she found out what he did, his whole life would be in her hands. He could lose his job, which was his life next to his daughter.

Kal pulled in the driveway and got out of his car. He saw the door to the house open and out came Kalsha.

She beamed and clapped her little hands together. "Daddy!" she exclaimed and ran into his arms.

Kal bent down, swooped her up in his arms and hugged her fiercely. Then he kissed her forehead. He looked into her eyes and saw Shana's eyes. After seeing her today, he knew Kalsha was the spitting image of her mother. He knew then he could not let the two of them ever meet, because if they did no one could miss the resemblance. It would be obvious they were mother and daughter.

"Kal, how was your day?" his sister, Sadie, asked walking out the door.

"Sis, even if I tell you, you are not going to believe it."

"Really. Try me."

"Shana is working at the hospital."

"No way! Are you serious?" she asked.

"Dead serious," Kal answered.

"Come in," she said opening the door to the house, "and tell me all about it."

"Can't wait," Kal said and sat down at the dining room table to confide in his best friend, his sister. "Where should I start?" Kal knew it was time to tell his sister the whole story and in reality, he was relieved to finally tell someone else. Shana's appearance had forced his hand. It would be good to confide in Sadie. He wasn't sure what was in the future for him and Kalsha.

"The beginning is always best." She sat down after sitting Kalsha down in the family room with her toys. "I'm listening."

* * * *

Desert Oasis Golf Club left a message on Shana's phone the next morning requesting the final count for the golf event. The problem was she didn't have the counts they needed. She needed to get them from the golf liaison doctor, which was Kal. Couldn't they wait until tomorrow? She didn't want to call Kal, at least not until after they had their meeting tonight. Shana called the Desert Oasis but was only able to confirm they needed the counts today and they couldn't wait until tomorrow. Damn. How was she going to get out of this? Finally, she opted to email Kal for the counts. Obviously, the chicken way out, nonetheless it would suffice. Kal promptly emailed her back the numbers and the names of all the doctors attending. Great. That was done.

The phone rang and she looked down to see Kal's name appear on the caller id. It rang a couple of times before she reached for it.

"This is Shana," she said.

"Kal. Just wanted to be sure you got my email with all the names for the golfers."

"Yes."

"Great. We're all set then?"

"I'll let you know if I need anything else."

"Sounds good. And I'll see you tonight at six at The Desert Rose."

"I'll be there."

"I'll see you later then."

"Okay," Shana said and hung up the phone. Well she'd survived that. Now hopefully she would survive tonight, too.

* * * *

Shana stood in front of her closet trying to decide what to wear. The day had flown by and before she knew it, it was five. Now she had only a few minutes to pick something to change into. Originally, she was going to wear the tan suit she'd worn to work, however decided to change into something less stuffy. She actually had no clue what she should wear. It wasn't actually a date. She wasn't really trying to attract his attention, was she? Hell, she didn't know if she was or not. Finally, she grabbed a pair of capri-length jeans, a low cut black tank top and some black-heeled sandals. She changed quickly, touched up her makeup and hair before leaving her apartment. Not wanting to be late, she arrived about five minutes early. She walked into The Desert Rose to see Kal already there talking to the hostess.

Kal turned to see her approach him. "There she is," Kal said to the hostess and smiled at Shana.

The hostess led them to a patio table with an umbrella. Music played in the background. The patio was surrounded by a make shift wall with planters of brilliant red roses on the top, providing privacy to the patrons.

"This is very nice," Shana said.

"Yes, it is. A friend of mine recommended it. I will have to thank him."

They both ordered a glass of wine. Then there was that awkward silence. Shana didn't know what to say and felt it was up to Kal to initiate a conversation so she waited.

Kal studied her across the table. Unfortunately, he certainly liked what he saw. How could he not when every time he looked into Shana's face he saw Kalsha's face, a face he loved and loved to look at.

Why? Why had she done it? That was what he wanted to ask. Unfortunately, he couldn't. Not unless she offered the information. So he decided to start at the beginning, since she was obviously waiting for him to start up a conversation. First, they would order dinner. He was not above wining and dining her to get the answers he needed.

The Desert Rose was a steakhouse so they both ordered steaks and salads. The waitress brought out their wine and a basket of breads and rolls, which they snacked on in silence.

Finally, Kal asked, "Do you remember the night we met?"

"Yes," Shana answered. "A night I will never forget."

"Why is that?" he asked.

You were my first and only one-night stand."

"A one-night stand, huh. I guess it turned out that way, didn't it?"

"Yes, it certainly did."

"That's not what I intended," Kal said honestly.

"What did you intend then?" Shana asked, as anger unintentionally surfaced on her face.

"When I saw you sitting at the bar, I thought you were beautiful and I wondered if I even stood a chance with you. My ego engulfed my thoughts and I approached you. I really didn't expect you to be receptive to me. Figured you were probably already taken."

"I figured you looked too good to be hitting on me. I rarely go to bars and even more rare that I went alone," Shana offered.

"What made you decide to go there alone?" Kal asked, wanting to understand her motives better.

"I got laid off from my job of ten years that day. It was completely unexpected. I never saw it coming."

"I see. But you didn't say anything about it."

"I think I was in shock. Plus, I don't really drink and I'd had two drinks already when you came up to talk to me."

"Are you saying you were drunk by then?"

"One is my limit, and I was starting my third."

"I see."

"No, I don't think you do. Not only had I lost my job, I'd buried my mother only three months prior."

"I'm sorry," Kal said.

"That's not even all of it. Mother had been sick for over a year before she died. I was responsible for all the medical bills."

"Don't you have any other family?" Kal asked.

"No," Shana answered as her eyes watered.

Kal realized he'd opened a fresh wound as she thought of her dead parents.

"Needless to say, I was in bad shape. I really needed that job, and I really needed to be with someone that night. It had been two years since my divorce."

"You hadn't had sex for two years?" Kal asked, not that it was so unusual to go without sex, but it was personal. He wanted to know if she'd been with anyone else.

"Yes, it wasn't so much the sex I wanted—not that it wasn't great, because it was," Shana said. Kal observed her as she continued, "I simply wanted to be held."

"That I understand. It had been a year since my breakup with my fiancée," Kal offered. He looked into her eyes and continued, "I, too, wanted to hold a woman and be held."

"So both of our needs were satisfied. I guess you were just looking for a one-night stand?" Shana asked directly.

"Why do you say that?"

"Well, I never heard from you again."

"You gave me your business card, remember?" Kal asked.

"Yes."

"I called your work place; however you were no longer employed there." Kal recalled his disappointment that day.

"I wrote my home number on the card," Shana said waiting for his reply.

"When I got back from conference, I called but it was disconnected."

"Sorry, I forgot I was moving that same weekend."

"I know. I came over to your apartment and they said you moved, and they couldn't give out any information as to where."

"Oh," Shana said.

Kal noticed regret on her face and wondered…"I'm going to be perfectly honest at this point. I don't make it a habit of having one-night stands either. Initially, I intended our night to be just that—one night. Although I enjoyed our evening together, I wasn't going to call you. However, I couldn't stop thinking about you while I was at the conference. So I decided to call you and see if you were interested in going out again, and see where it went from there. Unfortunately you'd disappeared."

"I'm sorry. I didn't know you'd tried to find me. I never heard from you so I figured you didn't want to see me again. You never gave me your business card, or number, so I had no way of finding you with only a first name."

Kal studied her face as she spoke, seeing the underlying pain, sensing her realization of how different things could've been if she'd had his number. "You have no idea how much I regretted not giving you my business card."

"That brings me to the money you left me. Why?"

"Like I said, I initially planned on having a one-night stand with you. It's not something I felt comfortable with so I wanted to give you something to make up for that. So you could buy yourself something."

Taking Chances

"It made me feel like you paid me for sex."

"No, I didn't mean it to be taken like that," Kal explained, realizing what he'd done without intending to.

"It made me feel like a whore," Shana blurted out.

Kal could see the hurt in her eyes. "I am so sorry, that was not my intention." He could see now that he'd caused her tremendous pain at a time when she was already barely staying above her maximum pain threshold to remain at a functional level.

Their salads were set out before them and they both ate in silence.

Kal watched Shana through different eyes. She'd been hurt terribly by his actions. She'd had some difficult decisions to make all alone. Finally, he asked, "So did you find another job?" Ah shit, why'd he asked that? He knew the answer!

"Not for about a year. I got very depressed after that night with everything else that had happened."

"You mean losing the job and your mother?" He didn't think she'd say anything about the pregnancy still he had to see.

"Yes. I had to live on unemployment, had no money for medical so it took a while to get through the depression. I finally ended up going through counseling at a free clinic and took a part time job at Starbucks."

Kal's heart went out to her. Her life had been difficult. He felt quite confident she didn't know about Kalsha though.

Her blonde hair framed her face and her golden eyes were mesmerizing. Her top was cut low and he had a nice view of her cleavage. Hell, she turned him on. There was just this huge dark cloud though that was hanging over them, and they couldn't go anywhere until it was gone. He couldn't tell her that he had their baby daughter, and he was damn sure she wasn't going to tell him about the terminated pregnancy.

They ate and Kal chatted with her about the hospital and Phoenix. She talked about Minneapolis and how glad she was to be here where it was warm. The server brought the dessert tray out for them to look at.

"Go ahead and pick one," he said.

"Oh, I don't know. They all look so good." Shana eyed them all.

Kal laughed, "Okay, pick two and we'll share."

"The chocolate indulgence and the cheesecake with fresh berries," she said to the server.

"Good choices," Kal said and smiled at her.

After dessert, there was a deafening silence. Shana was at a loss for words. What did one say at this point? She stared at his chiseled tan face. He was so extremely good looking, and the attraction to him was strong. Damn! She needed to leave.

"Well, I think it's time to call it a night," Shana said as she got up from the table.

"I know this was a bit awkward at first, but hopefully it was helpful for both of us to talk about that night. Especially since it appears, we both attempted to do that back then. For some unknown reasons, it didn't work out." Kal stood up and they walked to the door.

"Having my unanswered questions answered was greatly appreciated," Shana said, stopping outside the door.

"I know we can't go back, though maybe we can be friends, at least, since we'll be working at the hospital together. What do you think?" Kal asked offering his hand.

"Friends," Shana said, extended her hand and shook Kal's. She hesitated a moment to look into his eyes.

Kal wanted to kiss her but knew he couldn't so he released her hand and backed away.

"See you at the hospital," Kal said and continued backing up towards the parking lot.

"Thanks for the dinner," Shana replied.

"It was the least I could do." Kal turned and walked away.

Shana walked to her car. Her heart felt lighter than it had in years. Her questions had been answered. She hadn't been totally honest with him, yet sometimes it was best to not bring up something that couldn't be undone. No matter what she said or did, it would not change the fact she'd terminated the pregnancy. Nothing could bring back the child they'd made together.

Chapter Eight

Kal got into his car and watched Shana get into hers. He knew he should've been a gentleman and escorted her out to the parking lot, but he couldn't. Those luscious, alluring lips were too tempting and he almost kissed them when they shook hands. Lord only help him what might have happened if he'd walked her to the car.

What was wrong with him? He was behaving like a high school boy, barely able to keep his hormones in check. She was a beautiful, attractive woman. Sitting across the table from her, catching glimpses of firm, perfectly formed breasts when she leaned forward almost undid him. He'd had a hard on almost through the entire dinner. It took all the willpower he had to keep control of his urges so he could walk out of the restaurant without embarrassing himself. Why she had this effect on him, after all this time, he had no idea. All he knew was she did and he wanted her even more after tonight.

She'd redeemed herself some in his eyes, knowing she'd been expecting him to call. After she explained her situation at the time regarding her losses, he actually felt sorry for her. And to top it off, he felt guilty. For the first time in two years, he felt like he was partially responsible for what happened. Like the pregnancy. He really couldn't blame her solely; he would have to accept part of the blame. They'd both drank too much, and neither had been thinking clearly.

Why hadn't he left his business card with the fifty dollars? Because he was being controlling, that's why. It was going to be his choice, and only his choice, if they saw each other again. That had turned out well, hadn't it? If he hadn't tried to be so macho, she would've had his number to call him and tell him she was pregnant. As for the pregnancy, wasn't he the one who'd had unprotected sex? Hell, he was a doctor, he should have known better, except he'd been drunk. Although that was no excuse for not using a condom. He, of course, had assumed she was on the pill. Yet had he asked? No he hadn't. He'd assumed.

Then, of course, there was the fact that if he'd called her the next day instead of waiting a week, he'd have gotten a hold of her. God only knew, he'd wanted to call her that day. Hell, he couldn't stop thinking about her. Making love to her. Being a guy, he'd figured it was just because he hadn't had sex with a woman for over a year. Hand jobs in the shower simply weren't the same as a warm blooded, sexy woman.

This could've turned out entirely different. He could've been married to Shana and raised their baby together. He could be a married man with a wife and baby. Having Shana as his wife wouldn't be bad at all. Unfortunately things hadn't happened that way, and he would have to try to steer clear of her as much as possible since this attraction was so strong, yet couldn't go anywhere.

* * * *

"Kal, how'd it go?" Sadie asked, giving him the eye as he walked through the door.

"It was revealing," Kal said, looking around for Kalsha.

"She's sleeping. Now tell me how it was revealing," Sadie demanded.

"The night I met Shana, she'd been laid off of her job of ten years a few hours earlier," Kal stated.

"She must've been devastated."

"I didn't know. She never said anything that night."

"Poor woman," Sadie said sympathetically.

"That's not all. Her mother died a couple months earlier, leaving her with huge medical bills to pay."

"Oh my! That poor woman."

"The following Saturday she moved. I never gave her my business card so she couldn't call me."

"You two are star crossed lovers," Sadie said.

Taking Chances

"I see now that I have to accept some of the blame for what happened. This wasn't all her fault. And damn it, I should've used a condom!"

"At this point, I can't agree with that. If you had, we wouldn't have your beautiful daughter, Kalsha," Sadie answered thoughtfully.

"Who happens to be the spitting image of her mother."

"Do you have feelings for her?"

"Unfortunately, that may be the case. I am certainly attracted to her. I probably could fall in love with Shana if given the chance."

"So what are you going to do?"

"Stay as far away from her as I can," Kal stated emphatically.

* * * *

Shana drove home barely seeing the streets as she drove. Her mind was fully occupied with Kal. She had to admit, she didn't actually hate him anymore. She needed to talk to someone. More than ever, she wished she could talk to her mother. They'd always been so close. Her mother would've known the right things to say to comfort her.

Shana was restless when she got home. She really needed to talk to someone about what just happened. Tara. Yes, she would send her an email. She turned on her laptop and started the email. After only a few sentences, she checked the time. It was a little after seven, so it was only after nine in Minneapolis. Did she dare call Tara? Tara had said she could call anytime. She needed to talk to Tara, so she picked up her cell and called.

"Hello," Tara answered.

"Hope it's not too late," Shana said.

"Shana! No, it's fine. How'd your meeting with Kal go tonight?"

"I'm glad I went. I really need to talk to you about it. Do you have time now?"

"Sure. I'm anxious to hear. So did he answer your questions?"

"Yes, he did."

"Well, tell me what he said," Tara prompted.

"He said initially he intended to have just a one-night stand."

"Initially? But he never contacted you again. How does that work?" Tara asked.

"He left that morning for a conference and called when he got back."

"Called where? You never got a call."

"I'd given him my business card, so he called Ultimate Promotions, looking for me."

"Oh."

"My home phone was on the back, so he called that too, however it was disconnected because I'd moved that weekend."

"That's right. I'm so sorry, Shana."

"That's not even all of it. He went to my apartment and found I'd moved. The apartment said they couldn't give out any forwarding information."

"So, then he gave up," Tara summarized.

"Yes, can't actually blame him at that point."

"Did you ask him about the fifty dollars?"

"Yes. He thought he only wanted a one-night stand, so he didn't leave a business card and left the money as a gift so I could buy myself something."

"So he was feeling guilty and it was to make himself feel better about what he'd done," Tara evaluated, the counselor in her coming through.

"I guess so."

"Obviously, he must've changed his mind since he tried to find you."

"He said he couldn't stop thinking about me at his conference," Shana replied.

"Really. Do you believe him?"

"Yes, I guess so. He seemed sincere."

"He say anything else?"

"After the discussion, there didn't seem to be anything else to talk about. There was a lot of silence and it was rather awkward. Thankfully, the food came shortly."

"So you had a nice meal then?" Tara asked, probing for more.

"Yes. We even ordered two desserts."

"Did you two talk more?"

Taking Chances

"Just talked about Minneapolis, Phoenix and the hospital. But then—"

"What?" Tara asked.

"When we were leaving, he almost kissed me."

"Really? Are you sure?"

"Well, it certainly seemed that way," Shana stated.

"Did you want him to kiss you?"

"I think so. He is so attractive. Such a fit body with a chiseled, tanned face. And his eyes!" Shana recalled.

"Okay, so you are attracted to him. Now what?"

"A part of me would love to pursue a relationship with him, but—"

"You're afraid."

"He would never understand what I did or forgive me."

"How do you know?" Tara asked.

"I don't. I just don't think we could get past it so there is no point," Shana said.

"Still you don't know, so there is a possibility."

"Can't."

"Shana, you don't have to make any decisions tonight. You can wait and see what happens," Tara suggested.

"We agreed to be friends," Shana stated.

"Friends?"

"Yes. Be polite to each other around the hospital, etc."

"Oh. That would be good since you have to work together. Or at least somewhat work together," Tara stated.

"What do you think I should do, Tara?"

"I think you just need to take a day at a time and see what happens. It's up to him what happens next. Unfortunately, guys always have the upper hand there. So just wait and see. That is, of course, if you want anything to happen."

"That's the big question, isn't it?"

"If you don't want anything more to do with him, simply ignore him. He'll get the message and leave you alone."

"Then again what if I do, but know it can't go anywhere?" Shana asked.

Rose Marie Meuwissen

"That's a decision you may have to make. Whether you would like to find out or not," Tara offered.

"Do you think there is any chance for us after what happened?"

"Shana, there is always a chance no matter what the odds are. Nonetheless it's probably best to keep your expectations low and see what happens."

"Okay, that makes sense. I'll give it a try. It certainly helped talking to you, Tara. Thanks."

"No problem. Keep me informed on how it is going."

"I will. I'll let you go now because I know it's late there. I'll call if anything happens," Shana promised, and ended the call feeling much better.

* * * *

Everything was going as planned for the golf event. Only one more day until the big day, Friday. Thankfully, she hadn't really had to talk to Kal much. Only a few emails had taken care of the information she needed from him. She knew she was a bit more stressed than usual however that was because she wanted everything to be perfect. Mainly, so Kal would see that she was good at what she did. She wanted to make a good impression. She didn't have high hopes anything would happen between her and Kal, yet she still wanted to look good to him. Kal hadn't approached her at the hospital since their sort of date, although she knew she would see him tomorrow. Yes, and there would be interactions then.

"I've got everything boxed up that we need to take to the golf course tomorrow," Meg said.

"Great. I think we're all set then," Shana replied.

"I'll drop off the list for the team tee offs at the golf course on my way home. See you in the morning then."

"Enjoy your evening, Meg," Shana called out as Meg left.

Shana finished turning off everything, deciding to call it a day. She wanted to get plenty of rest for the big event tomorrow. Not that the golf event was such a big event, though spending the day with Kal was. On the way home, she stopped for her nail and pedicure appointment. She had her clothes all laid out for tomorrow—a salmon Capri pantsuit

Taking Chances

and matching sandals. She was going to make sure Kal didn't find her lacking in the visual category at the very least. It was their past history category that was an issue.

* * * *

The next morning, Shana awoke to bright sunshine, as was the usual status quo for Phoenix. She felt refreshed and eager to meet this day head on with enthusiasm. Thankfully, she'd slept well due to the Sleepy Time herbal tea she'd drank before going to bed. Phoenix had proven good for Shana. Her mood and outlook on life was elevated by simply being there. Seeing the sun each morning made a huge difference to her day.

She took extra care to be sure her eye make-up and hair were perfect before she left. Done and pleased, she took one final look in the mirror. Happy with what she saw, she left and headed out to her daylong appointment with Kal. Not really, yet it could certainly turn out that way.

After stopping by the hospital, Shana and Meg carried the boxes out to their cars and drove to the golf course to get everything set up. Tee offs had already started at seven. Thankfully, their clubhouse contact had offered to get the early golfers started for her. Shana knew Kal had opted for a tee off at nine, so she knew she wouldn't see him until after the first nine holes were done. Shana and Meg were so organized it didn't take long for them to get set up. The teams would turn in their score sheets after the first nine and then break briefly for a lunch of hamburgers, brats and beer. Then head out to complete the last nine holes.

Since Shana and Meg finished so quickly, they decided to take a break and sit on the restaurant patio and enjoy a cold glass of lemonade. The patio had an excellent view of the golf course. You could see the golf carts and golfers out on the golf course, although it was impossible to make out any faces. The greens were a lush green with scattered ponds of water and palm trees. It didn't look like the golf courses in Minnesota, still it was a beautiful sight. There was a gentle breeze blowing on them. Shana reached up to brush the hair back from her face. It felt so relaxing to simply sit there taking in the view. Meg was talking about a past golf tournament she'd worked on, but Shana was only half listening. Her mind was on Kal, and she found herself wondering which green he was on.

About eleven, the teams started coming in for lunch. Shana and Meg sat at the check in table located in the Clubhouse lobby, collecting the scorecards. The men were very pleasant and talkative, eager to brag about their great drives or putts. She listened politely but kept her eye on the door, so she would know when Kal was back. Eventually his tall, trim figure framed the door. Her eyes were glued on him and as her eyes moved up and focused on his face, she realized he was looking at her also. He smiled and walked towards her table.

"Hi," Kal said, handing her his team's scorecard.

"Hi." Shana took his scorecard.

"How's our tournament going?"

"Great. Everything is going as planned."

"It's a beautiful day," Kal said, staring at Shana and, since he was standing and she was sitting down, she realized he had a titillating partial view of her breasts. "And if I may say, you look beautiful, too."

"Thank you," Shana managed to stammer out. He was still staring at her. "You can help yourself to the buffet lunch out on the patio."

"Yes, I'll do that." Kal walked to the patio where the rest of the guys were eating. *Had he actually just said that to her? What was the matter with him?* It certainly wasn't his brain he was thinking with when he was around her, that's for sure.

By the time all the teams checked in, Kal was finished eating and already golfing the back nine. Thank heavens he was gone, Shana thought. He'd certainly unnerved her by what he'd said and his reaction to her. Only after he'd left did she realize he'd had a full view of her breasts from where he'd stood. How embarrassing! Meg had only laughed and said, "Way to go." That was probably justified since she'd dressed specifically for him today. He appreciated the visual and wasn't that what she wanted?

After all the teams were back out golfing, Shana and Meg finished calculating where the teams ranked, and they walked out to the patio to have lunch. They took their time because it would be a couple hours before the first teams finished their last nine holes. At least it gave her time to recoup from her last conversation with Kal. Yes, recoup. She needed to be ready to talk to him again when they got back in.

The teams started coming back in a little later. She and Meg collected the scorecards as the men retreated to the patio bar for drinks and cigars. One of Kal's teammates brought the scorecard for his team over to Shana. She looked out to the patio and saw Kal sitting at a table with both a drink and cigar. So he must be avoiding her this time. That's okay; she'd see him at dinner.

After all the team scores were tallied, they listed their first, second and third place teams, along with the longest drive and putt winners. She and Meg walked to the ballroom to get situated for the dinner. They only had an hour yet almost everything was done. As soon as the bar was ready, Meg went out to the patio bar to steer the men towards the ballroom. Shana finished up details with the kitchen as the men began to file into the room. Kal came up to the microphone, welcomed all the players, and congratulated them on an excellent day of golf. Kal then took his seat at the table and right on cue, the servers began serving the meal.

The dinner was excellent. Everyone appeared to be having a nice time. It was almost time for the awards and prizes. Kal would present these and she would help. Shana looked up to see Kal approaching her table.

"Ready?" Kal asked.

"Yes," Shana answered, gathering up her papers. She rose, followed Kal to the podium, and handed him a sheet of paper. "Here is the list for you to go by."

"Thanks," Kal said, as his eyes lingered on her face and he smiled appreciatively. "Let's do it," he said.

Shana watched his charisma work the group. He was an extremely entertaining speaker, engaging all while he spoke. On cue, she handed him the envelopes containing the prizes for the winners. After that, they were done.

"Nice job, Shana. The golf tournament turned out great, thanks to you," Kal said reaching to shake her hand.

"Thanks, I think it turned out well." Shana shook his hand, however, as soon as their hands touched, she could feel the spark ignite between them. Her gut reaction was to pull her hand back, but before she could react, one of the men called to Kal to meet them on the patio. She felt his hand reluctantly slide from hers.

"Got to go," Kal said and started walking towards the patio. He stopped and turned back towards Shana. "Catch you later." He gave her a smile and then proceeded to join the other men seated on the patio with their drinks to rehash their day.

"Well, that's that," Shana said watching his retreating back.

"What did you say?" Meg asked walking up.

"Nothing important."

"Right," Meg said.

Shana caught Meg's ironic tone and said, "Let's get all of our stuff together so we can get out of here."

They were able to make it in one trip. It was such a beautiful night, Shana didn't really want to go home yet and, since she was looking exceptionally hot tonight, even if she did say so herself, she said, "Meg, do you know any exciting local hang-outs where we could stop and have a glass of wine?"

"Thought you'd never ask. There's one a few blocks from here. Very upscale with nice looking, available men."

"Sounds perfect. I'll follow you."

They pulled up to The McCormick Ranch in Scottsdale. It was a Friday night so it was bustling with young professionals. They lucked out and grabbed a table near the bar. The bar had live bands on the weekend and a local band just started playing.

"What do you think?" Meg asked.

"This is great. Do you know the band?" Shana asked.

"Yes, I've heard them play before. They're good and easy to dance to."

The band began playing and the two women listened, talked and drank their wine. Meg knew a few people who had stopped by their table to talk briefly. The music was rock with some songs upbeat and some slow and relaxing. Meg went out to dance with a friend she knew. Shana watched the band and scanned the crowd. Then she heard *his* voice—Kal.

Taking Chances

She turned towards the entrance and saw him and a few of the other doctors walk in. She quickly turned back towards the band. Why she'd turned away, she wasn't sure. She could still hear his voice so she knew he was close. She turned back quickly to see where he was. Sure enough, he was sitting at the bar behind her. She decided he hadn't noticed her yet. She couldn't wait until Meg got back.

"Sorry, didn't mean to leave you here alone so long. I know that sucks," Meg said returning to her seat, which was facing the bar.

"I'm fine," Shana said.

"Say, isn't that Dr. Paxton at the bar?" Meg asked trying to focus better on the bar now that there were people standing between their table and the bar.

"Yes," Shana said. "Maybe we should go?"

"Why? We were here first. It's not like we followed him here. No, it's more the other way around. Do you think he saw us?" Meg asked.

"No, I don't think he saw us."

"Really. Well, I think you're wrong because he's coming over here right now."

"Great," Shana muttered. She could feel him standing behind her.

"Hi, ladies," Kal said. "What a coincidence we all chose the same bar."

"Yes, isn't it? Meg suggested it," Shana said.

The other three doctors joined them at the table.

"Mind if we sit with you two?" Kal asked, seeing the empty chairs.

"Of course not," Meg answered for them.

Kal took the chair next to Shana before any of the others had a chance.

The conversation centered on the day's golf event. The men bragged about their games and complimented Shana and Meg on how smoothly the event went.

Meg and one of the other doctors went out to dance, then Kal turned to Shana. "Would you like to dance?"

Chapter Nine

Did she dare dance with him? Shana hesitated.

"It's only a dance," Kal coaxed.

"I know. It's just so—Deja vu," Shana managed to get out.

"Sometimes you simply have to let go and live a little. Take a chance," Kal said. He stood up and reached for her hand.

Shana got up and walked to the dance floor with Kal. She didn't want to create a scene by saying no, yet she wasn't sure if by agreeing she'd unwittingly given cause for the gossip chain at the hospital to start up about them. *And taking chances? Hadn't she been there, done that?*

It was a fast dance, which would work out fine. Her body began to sway to the music. This could be fun. She would simply forget Kal was there and let her body be one with the music. She liked dancing, the way it made her feel free and one with the music. It also made her feel sexy and, to be honest, it turned her on. She lost herself to the music and words of the song and smiled at Kal. She could tell he was enjoying watching her body move. *Maybe this wasn't a wise decision after all.*

The song ended quickly and smoothly blended right into the next one—a slow song. Kal gave her a questioning look, moving closer, pulling her into his arms and pressing their bodies together. She didn't say anything or back away, so at that point there wasn't actually anything to do except put her arms around him and yes, touch him. Slow dancing could be extremely erotic if you were attracted to the other person. And if you had chemistry, there was no telling what could happen. They obviously had both. Her body was on fire for him. Her breasts tingled where they pressed against his firm chest.

She'd removed her jacket shortly after sitting at the table when she and Meg arrived at the bar because she was warm. It was a good thing, because now she was hot, and in more ways than one. Her low cut tank top allowed Kal an excellent, though unintentional view of her breasts. Her breasts tingled, aching for his mouth to pleasure them by sucking each one slowly with expertise. She looked up to see his eyes fixated on her breasts. If he only knew what she was wishing he would do to them.

She was being completely and totally reckless. Not that anything was going to happen. Not now, anyway. She felt his hand on her low back, flirting so very close to her butt, pull her ever so close to his body, teasing her with his erection—rock hard, pushing firmly against her pelvis. Thank God, they were in a public place so nothing else could happen. This time.

Thankfully, she was on the Pill. She'd started taking it about a year ago, because she was not going to get herself pregnant unexpectedly ever again. After all, she was a warm-blooded woman who had needs. She knew it had been way too long since she'd been held in the arms of a man. She wondered if he had any idea she hadn't been with anyone else since the last time they'd been together. He was a guy. He'd probably been with women since that night. She wanted him to make love to her again, and she wanted to be sober this time so she could completely enjoy it. All night long.

She looked up into his face again. His eyes were dark and glazed. She wanted to touch his lips with her finger and then brush her lips gently over them, then hungrily devour his mouth with hers.

The song ended and his mouth moved towards her. His lips gently touched hers and deepened quickly. He stopped abruptly. They were on the dance floor surrounded by people. Some of which were their coworkers. Damn!

"I'm sorry," Kal said. "I shouldn't have done that."

"Right ..." Shana said, pulling back to put some distance between them. She turned and walked back to the table.

No one at the table said a word.

"See you all at the hospital," Kal said, walking up behind her. He gave Shana a quick nod and left.

"I'm going to the ladies room," Shana said to Meg.

"Me, too," Meg said and followed Shana. Catching up, she asked, "Everything okay?"

"Yes, why?"

"You and Kal acted strange when you came back."

"Did you see us on the dance floor?" Shana asked.

"Dancing? Yes," Meg answered.

"Slow dancing?" Shana questioned.

"Yes."

"I need to know if you or any of the doctors saw Kal kiss me." Shana stared into Meg's eyes.

"I think I was the only one looking towards you when the song ended. Kal's back was facing our way so I couldn't tell what was happening. It just looked like you were talking," Meg replied.

"Oh—" Shana said.

"He kissed you? I could tell he likes you."

"Great. Just what I need."

"You don't like him?"

"I didn't say that," Shana answered quickly.

"But you let him kiss you?" Meg wondered.

"It just happened."

"Okay, my lips are sealed," Meg, stated.

"Promise?" Shana asked, with pleading in her voice.

"I promise."

"I'm going home." Shana left the ladies room, headed straight out the entrance door to the parking lot and her car.

What the Hell was she thinking to let that happen? Let him kiss her? On a dance floor in front of co-workers? She was embarrassed. She was trying so hard to start her life over and make a good impression. Now what had she done? Meg didn't think anyone saw it. So maybe it was fine. Meg knew now only because she'd told her. What a fool! She should've kept her mouth shut, but she needed to know. Could she trust Meg? She hoped so, however she didn't know because she hadn't known Meg for very long. Enough. There wasn't anything she could do about it now, anyway. It had happened. Kal had initiated it; so it was his fault not hers. Oh, who cared whose fault it was anyways? No one.

What she needed to focus on was what happened between the two of them. Was he attracted to her still? It certainly appeared he was. His body had reacted to hers as much as hers had to his. Damn! She'd wanted to feel his naked body against her naked body. The sexual feelings she had for him were so strong. She so did not want to have another one-night stand though. She wanted to have a loving relationship, one that would last. He was not the one for that. They had bad history. A one-night stand that started out on a night just like tonight. Not that the night back then was so bad. Hell, neither was tonight. It's just the first one ended with dire circumstances later down the line.

Tonight had taken her to a place she didn't want to go again. And if they proceeded with trying to have a relationship, she would have to tell him and she just couldn't. If she ever told him the consequences of their one night together, he would no longer want anything to do with her, so it was best not to start anything. She simply had to figure out how to extinguish the fire burning within her body for him. Kal. She needed to talk to him about it. He hadn't given her a chance tonight. *Come to think of it, why had he left so quickly?*

* * * *

Kal got to his car and took deep breaths to calm down before he exploded. Damn! What had he just done? His fist slammed down on the dash of his car. His body was primed; he was rock hard and wanted her. He was going utterly insane. That was the only possible conclusion.

As soon as he'd watched her sexy, trim body move to the rhythm of the music and gazed down at those firm tan breasts swaying before his eyes, he was on fire. He had an instant hard on. When his body touched hers, pressed against her, he was a goner. He'd put his hand as far down her back as he dared. A few inches more and he would've reached her sweet, perfect butt. While they danced, he could see the passion in her eyes when she looked up at him. The dance was going to end soon at that point and he hadn't wanted to let her go.

Hell, what he wanted was to take her home with him and make love to her luscious, sexy body. Her breasts spilled slightly over her low tank top and he wanted to look at her nipples taut and ripe, waiting to be suckled. By him. He wanted to move down her flat stomach to her belly button and continue moving down to the heat of her body. And then those full, inviting lips were there for the taking. He couldn't help himself, he had to kiss them. So he did.

It was everything he remembered it would be. Shana hadn't resisted either. Hell, he knew her body wanted his, too. He could feel the need in her. She was his for the taking. If he wanted her. That was the real question. Did he want another one-night stand? He knew he wanted more than that. He wanted to have a real relationship. One including love, sex and companionship. He wanted a mother for his child. Could he possibly have that with Shana, the mother of his child? No, that was the problem. He could probably have it all with Shana, but yet he couldn't. He just couldn't. Not with her. Not after what she'd done. She hadn't said anything about it to him the other night either.

How did one broach a topic no one wanted to talk about? Hell, he didn't know. Could they even possibly talk about what happened? There was so much at stake. He thought he could never have feelings for her, although after tonight, he was well aware of the fact that he did indeed have sexual feelings for her. He saw Kalsha every time he looked at Shana. The resemblance was uncanny.

How could he love one and not the other? He knew the answer however he didn't want to accept the truth, which was he couldn't. Naturally, he would love both. Damn! He had to stay away from her. Hell, she was probably mad at him for kissing her in public, anyway. Then he'd left without saying anything to her. Hopefully, she was mad as Hell and wouldn't want anything else to do with him. Hopefully. Hell, he prayed she wouldn't.

Later, Kal arrived at his sister's house and as he walked in swore, "Damn!"

"Kal?" Sadie questioned.

"I've absolutely lost my mind."

Taking Chances

"Would you care to tell me what you're going on about? And try to be a bit quieter. Kalsha is sleeping." Sadie pointed to the bedroom where Kalsha slept peacefully.

"I kissed her," Kal stated point blank.

"Who?" Sadie asked, puzzled.

"Shana."

"Oh ... well that explains everything," Sadie said.

"Exactly."

"I'm assuming she didn't force you to kiss her."

"No. It was my idea."

"Then you wanted to, right?" Sadie questioned.

"At the moment it seemed like the thing to do," Kal confessed.

"So what's the problem?" Sadie laughed, giving her baby brother the *look*.

"Don't look at me that way, Sadie. And don't laugh, it's not funny. This is serious."

"Oh, it's serious now, huh."

"No, it's not. You know what I mean. I had a momentary lapse in judgment," Kal stated.

"So what did Shana do?" Sadie asked.

"Nothing."

"In other words she kissed you back?" Sadie prompted with a question.

"Sort of."

"If she didn't slap you, she was probably okay with it."

"Who knows! I'm not okay with it. That's the problem," Kal said in a raised voice.

"I see."

"I'm the problem. I'm an idiot!"

"I wouldn't go that far," Sadie said, laughing again.

"I don't know what's wrong with me when I'm around her."

"You're obviously attracted to her."

"Obviously, and I don't know why. I should hate her."

"Do you?"

"I thought I did. I'm so damn attracted to her. When I'm near her, I can't think straight."

85

"You did say she is a beautiful woman, didn't you?"

"Absolutely! She's got a hot body any guy would kill to touch," Kal stated bluntly.

"Okay …So then you're normal because you want her."

"She has long blonde hair that frames her beautiful face and mesmerizing golden brown eyes. Just like Kalsha," Kal confessed.

"It's completely normal to love the mother of your child," Sadie stated.

"I don't love her and she certainly hasn't been a mother in any way."

"Maybe, she needs a second chance."

"Maybe, I just need to stay the Hell away from her."

"It's your life," Sadie said.

"Get Kalsha, I need to go home."

* * * *

It seemed like everywhere in the hospital he went today, he saw her. Shana. He just couldn't get away from her. Not that she'd sought him out or anything. Well, she certainly wasn't doing a very good job, but then again she hadn't approached him either. She'd only waved his way once and then left quickly down a different hall. He had the distinct feeling she was avoiding him. He wasn't sure why, nonetheless it annoyed him. He actually felt somewhat insulted by her actions.

What was wrong with him? Shouldn't she jump at the chance to go out with a doctor who was a down to earth nice guy, too? *So what was her problem?*

Shana had a lot to hide from him, like the pregnancy. She probably didn't want to have that discussion with him. He couldn't completely blame her. But then again he hadn't asked her out, had he? No, he hadn't given her the option to say yes or no. It was best not to go there anyway, so he would continue trying to avoid her.

* * * *

She'd almost run into him in the hall again. It was a close call. All day, Monday, she'd been trying her best to avoid Kal unfortunately it seemed everywhere she went, he was. There simply wasn't any way they could have a future together so she needed to steer clear of him.

Taking Chances

It was almost time to go home and she'd managed not to run into Kal anymore. Rounding the last hallway corner leading to the parking lot, she stopped abruptly. Kal was standing at the door talking with another doctor. They both looked her way before the other doctor left through the door. Kal stared at her as if he didn't have the faintest idea what to do or say. She kept walking towards him. What else could she do? Stop? And do what? No, she had no alternative but to keep walking and talk to him as briefly as possible.

"Hi," Shana said stopping at the door where Kal stood watching her walk towards him. He was only being polite, she reassured herself.

"Shana," Kal managed to get out.

Shana stared at him, waiting for him to say something.

"I think we should go out on a date," Kal stated, giving her his conclusion.

"A real date?" Shana questioned, not sure she heard him correctly.

"Yes."

"I don't—"

"We have unfinished business to take care of," Kal stated.

"What do you mean?" Shana asked, still not sure where he was going with this.

"We need to spend some time together and see what happens," Kal explained.

"Really," Shana said as her heart stood still. Did she dare? What would one date hurt? It probably wouldn't go any further than one date and maybe it would stop her from wondering what might've been.

"Pick you up Friday at six?" Kal asked.

"Okay," Shana replied. It was only one date. She could do this. He was intelligent and handsome. It would be fun. It just wasn't going anywhere after that.

"Email me your address and I'll see you then," Kal said. Other nurses and doctors were coming down the hall so they both left and walked alone to their cars.

Shana grinned as she walked to her car. She was going on a date with Kal. Who would've thought that would ever happen? Certainly not her. Who knew if they had anything in common or even if they would get along in a real relationship? She certainly didn't. They obviously were attracted to one another. That would not be a problem. However, the issue of her past pregnancy would. At least she thought it would be. There was no point in bringing it up if they weren't going to have a serious relationship.

She would have to send Tara an email to let her know what had happened today. Tara was truly the only one she could talk to about this. Tara usually didn't check her emails at night though, so she most likely wouldn't hear back until tomorrow.

* * * *

Kal felt almost giddy as he drove to Sadie's to pick up Kalsha. Sadie and he had always been close and could tell each other anything. Sadie had not been able to have children so far, although she was still trying. Sadie and her husband, Mac, were now trying in vitro fertilization. Because Sadie had no children of her own, she loved taking care of Kalsha. Of course, Sadie would love any child of Kal's as if it were her own. What was not to love about Kalsha? She was a happy beautiful child. Who happened to look exactly like her mother.

"Now I really did it," Kal said as he walked in. He could hear Kalsha playing in the living room.

"Did what?" Sadie asked, walking into the foyer to meet him.

"I tried not talking to her, which I almost managed do. I mean I did everything I could to avoid her all day and almost succeeded."

"Okay, now I am totally confused. Get to the point. What did you do? Kiss her again?" Sadie asked, fully lost as to what he was trying to say.

"No. Worse. Not only did I talk to her, I asked her out on a date," Kal admitted.

"Way to go, Dr. Stud," Sadie said, laughing.

"Don't call me that, Sis. You know I hate it."

"Well, so much for staying as far away from her as possible."

"I tried. Really, I did."

"So what happened?"

"I ran into her when I was leaving the hospital. When I looked at her, all I wanted to do was kiss her again," Kal said honestly.

Taking Chances

"So you did the next best thing and asked her out," Sadie concluded.

"I guess you might say that."

"Good."

"Good? Are you crazy? I should never have done it."

"Oh, well, it's over and done with now. So go with the flow as they say and plan a date she'll never forget."

"You think so? You think I should even go on the date? I could cancel at the last minute," Kal said as he paced the floor and ran his fingers through his hair.

"Oh, you're going all right. So start thinking about where you're taking her," Sadie ordered.

"I don't have any idea where to take her? I haven't been on a date for so long."

"I know. But you'll think of something." Sadie kissed her brother on the cheek. "I have confidence in you." She smiled and went to get Kalsha

Chapter Ten

The morning dragged as Shana checked her email again. Finally, there was one from Tara. She was eager to hear what Tara thought about her upcoming Friday night date with Kal.

The email read:

Shana,
In meetings all day, so this will be short. I think it's great! You should go. You two have unfinished business. Don't bring anything up about it yet. Just get to know each other and see if a relationship develops. The pregnancy is a topic for a much later conversation. So go and enjoy yourself!
Talk to you later, got to run. Let me know how it goes.
Tara

Shana sat back in her chair and released a deep sigh. Good. Tara thinks it's okay. Simply knowing that made her feel so much better. Tara was right; the pregnancy was for a later conversation.

She looked up as her computer dinged, signaling there was a new email. It was from Kal requesting her address and cell number in case he got lost on his way to her house. Giving him her address and cell number was a big step. She wasn't worried he would stalk her or anything. It's just those two things were very personal. She almost felt like they were actually going to be dating. Shana typed a reply and gave Kal her address and cell number. She clicked the send button.

Taking Chances

A few minutes later, Kal replied. He thanked her and reconfirmed the day and time. He also said to wear something dressy because they would be going to dinner at the Ocean Club restaurant in Scottsdale.

So he wasn't going to spare expense, he was going for high test. That was nice as long as he didn't expect sex in return. She wasn't ready yet. She was getting close though. She would need a strappy little black dress to wear. There really hadn't been any need to have one in her wardrobe the past couple of years so she would be going shopping after work. Hopefully, she could find one on a clearance rack at the mall.

Shana got up from her desk at five; she couldn't help the huge smile spreading across her face. It felt good to be going on a date. It had been way too long. Hell, she deserved some fun.

* * * *

Shana stared at the clearance rack full of dresses at Macys, a couple of hours later. Boy, had she lucked out! The rack was full of newly marked down dresses. After settling on ten dresses, she headed to the fitting room to try them on.

She walked out with an absolutely sexy strappy little black dress. It fit perfectly, hugging every inch of her body and framing her breasts with little black straps. The price was unbelievable—marked down 80%—and something she could never afford at regular price on her tight budget!

* * * *

Friday flew by at the hospital. Kal sent her a confirmation email stating he would pick her up at six. It was almost six and Shana was in her apartment just about ready. There were butterflies in her stomach. She was nervous. *Would he like the dress? Would he like the way she looked in the dress?* She had no idea what would happen. She would have to wait and see. Though not for long as moments later she heard a knock at the door.

Shana sprayed perfume on quickly, and slipped into her sandals before answering the door. "Kal, please come in," she said.

"You look beautiful," Kal commented, slowly taking in every delectable inch of Shana with his eyes as he stepped inside her apartment.

"I'll just get my purse." Shana smiled as she turned away.

Shana picked up her purse and locked the door on their way out. She waited while Kal opened the door to his Vet for her. Having a guy open a car door was always a pleasant surprise. Of course, it always said a lot about the guy.

Kal pulled up to the door of the Ocean Club to have the car valet parked. The valet opened Shana's door and helped her out of the car. She waited while Kal got out of the car and waited for the valet ticket. He walked up to her and they walked in together.

He'd called ahead for reservations and the table was ready—a cozy table for two with a view of the neighboring park gardens. It was a nice evening and the mahogany shuttered window doors were open. Shana sat down as the host held her chair out and seated her.

"This is lovely," Shana said.

"They have a reputation for having the best seafood in town," Kal said.

"So, I should order seafood?" Shana questioned.

"Unless you don't like seafood—"

"I love seafood," Shana said, laughing.

"Good, so do I," Kal said as the waiter appeared.

"Would you like some wine?" Kal asked.

"Yes, I'll have a glass of White Zinfandel," Shana said.

"We'll take a bottle of Beringer White Zinfandel," Kal said to the waiter.

Shana looked at the menu. The entrees were extremely expensive. However, Kal had chosen the restaurant so he must be able to afford it. Shana decided on a seafood trio plate featuring lobster, shrimp, and scallops. Kal ordered Halibut with an almond crust. The waiter brought the wine and breadbasket a few minutes later.

It was silent and awkward. Shana sipped her wine and took a piece of warm bread. She didn't say anything—it was his call. Kal sipped his wine and took a piece of bread. He was watching her.

Taking Chances

"So, Shana, what do you like to do in your spare time?" he asked a few minutes later.

"I like dancing, but don't get a chance to go very often. I was thinking about taking some Ballroom Dancing classes. It would probably be a good way to get out and meet people, too."

"It does seem to be quite popular these days. Especially with the television show, *Dancing with the Stars*."

"Have you ever thought about taking lessons?" Shana asked.

"Haven't thought about it. Although it could be fun. Especially Salsa," Kal answered.

"Yes, Salsa always looks like fun."

"We may have to check into some classes. It's probably better to go as a couple," Kal stated.

"What about you, what do you like to do?" Shana asked, changing the subject, since she had no response to his statement. *Was he actually suggesting they take classes together?*

"I like to golf. It gets me out and it's great exercise, too. Do you golf?"

"Yes, but I'm not very good."

"Maybe you just need some pointers. I could be of assistance in that regard," Kal offered.

"That would probably help me, along with more practice. I need to go more often."

The waiter brought their food order. Shana's seafood meal was extraordinary. Kal's halibut was light and flaky the way Halibut should be served. She knew because they'd tasted each other's food like real couples did.

"So what else do you like to do, Shana?"

"I like to read."

"What do you read?" Kal asked.

"No laughing, promise?"

"I promise," Kal said loving it when she smiled.

"Romance novels."

"Really. I know women like them. I see nurses reading them on their breaks and I always tease them about reading sex books."

"Well, they have sex in them, however they are love stories with happy endings."

"Do you think there are happy endings in real life?"

"I'm not sure. But I am open to the possibility. I keep hoping. That's what keeps me going."

The waiter brought the dessert tray out. Shana loved desserts and they all looked scrumptious. Chocolate was her favorite so she picked the lava cake—warm chocolate cake with melted chocolate on the inside served with a scoop of vanilla bean ice cream and then drizzled with chocolate syrup. Kal picked a piece of carrot cake—a whopping six layers with cream cheese frosting.

"What else do you like to do?" Shana asked.

"I like to watch movies, at the movie theater or at home on my big screen television."

"I like movies, too. Of course my choice would be a romantic comedy," Shana giggled.

"I would've never guessed."

"But I also like action movies."

The waiter placed the desserts on the table. Shana took a bite and felt like she was in heaven. "Oh! This chocolate is to die for! I haven't tasted chocolate this good in years."

Kal took a bite of his cake. "This is one of the best carrot cakes I've ever tasted. Their chefs are definitely to be commended."

The conversation turned to the everyday routines and gossip at the hospital. Kal filled her in on who was who on each floor. While they talked, the waiter presented the check and Kal handed him his credit card after briefly checking the total on the check.

After signing the receipt, they got up from the table and walked to the door. "Care to take a walk around the shopping plaza?" Kal asked.

"Sure, it's a nice night."

They walked side by side, stopping to stare in the windows of the stores at the large outdoor shopping plaza. Then walked into the well-groomed gardens in the park area and sat on a bench by a large stone water fountain.

Kal turned toward Shana and picked up her hands in his. He gently ran his thumb over the top of her hand. "Shana, I want to date you. I

Taking Chances

want to spend time with you, get to know you. I'm attracted to you immensely, nonetheless I want to take it slow and see if we have any chance at a future together."

Shana looked at his handsome, sun-bronzed face. He was so attractive and she felt mesmerized by his eyes and the sincerity in them. She wanted to do exactly what he'd just proposed yet she was scared to death. He obviously wanted her. He wanted this now but what about later when he found out what she'd done. His hand gently cupped her chin. His lips touched hers and then his tongue slid inside her mouth. He pulled her up close to his body. She was lost. Her arms went around his neck and she kissed him back passionately. A kiss filled with all the love and emotions bottled up inside her for over two years.

Kal pulled back a little to whisper in her ear, "Is that a yes?"

"Yes," Shana managed to get out and then his mouth was on hers again. His finger traced the strap of her dress along her shoulder. She pulled away a little. "You did say we'd go slowly, and I'm holding you to that." She gazed up at him.

"Yes, you're right." Kal stood and pulled her up. They walked back to the Ocean Club holding hands.

After the valet pulled the car up, Shana and Kal got in. They laughed and talked about movies they'd seen and ones they wanted to see on the drive back to Shana's apartment. Kal parked and walked Shana to her door. He held her hand as they walked up the steps.

"I'd like to take you to a movie tomorrow night."

"I'd like that," Shana said.

Now at her door, he turned her into his arms and kissed her with a breathtaking, intense kiss. He pressed her body against his, slid his hand down her back to her waist to the curve of her sweet little ass. His body was on fire. He wanted to pick her up in his arms, carry her to her bed, and make passionate love to her all night long. Instead, he broke the embrace and took a deep breath of fresh air.

"Okay, I promised slow, so I'll pick you up at five tomorrow and we'll grab a burger somewhere, then a movie," Kal said with glazed eyes still roaming over her body, even though his hands weren't.

"Sounds good," Shana said trying to regain her composure. It was a good thing he hadn't asked to come in because there was no way she could've said no.

Kal backed away towards the stairs, never taking his eyes off her. "You are so beautiful, and you have no idea how hard it is to walk away from you right now." With that, he turned and walked down the stairs. At the bottom, he paused, looked up at her and said, "Tomorrow at five."

Shana nodded, opened her door and went inside. As soon as she closed the door, she heard his car drive away.

"What a night!" Shana said out loud as a grin spread across her face and she collapsed on the couch full of hope and anticipation.

* * * *

Shana woke to bright sunshine. She loved this state with all its sun! She thought about Kal's kisses last night, and a huge smile spread across her face. She hadn't felt this happy in a long time. Lying in bed with her sexy teddy on, she thought about how good it would feel to have Kal's hands roaming her bare skin. It would feel good. Damn, but it would feel great! They had to go slow. She wanted a relationship, not just hot sex. Relationships took time. They had to get to know each other. Find out if they had any common interests. So far, they seemed to get along fine. So far, so good. The sexual attraction between them was intense, though. It made waiting hard. So just how long did they need to wait? Six weeks? Six dates? Six weeks seemed like a long time. More like forever when her body was on fire for him now. Six dates sounded better. More doable. They could still kiss and do some touching, of course. Six dates it was, she decided. If they still liked each other after six dates and still felt the attraction was there, she would allow Kal to make love to her. Again.

So was this date two or three they were going on tonight? Did the first dinner count? Sure, why not? They'd spent time together getting to know each other. So this was date three, and it was going to be fun. More talking. More getting to know each other. More kissing. More touching. She could hardly wait.

Taking Chances

That evening, she dressed in denim capris and a red tank top, Shana checked her appearance in the mirror as she put on her lipstick. Yes, she looked good. Her hair was up in a clip because it was a hot day and he would probably have the top down on the Vet. She'd spent the day cleaning up her apartment, doing laundry and managed a couple hours of reading time. She was anxious now to see Kal. It was a little before five and he should be there any minute.

* * * *

After dropping Kalsha back off at Sadie's, Kal drove to Shana's apartment. He had the top down on his Corvette and the wind was caressing his face as he drove. It had been a good day so far and the evening was going to be even better. He'd golfed early this morning with Mac. They had a standing second Saturday of the month golf tee off at eight. The afternoon was Kalsha's time. They'd gone to the park and had a picnic lunch packed by Sadie. Sadie was the best sister anyone could ask for. She took good care of Kalsha and him. He didn't know what he'd have done without her. Even though this afternoon she'd practically shoved him out the door after he dropped Kalsha off. She was probably more excited about him dating Shana than he was. Well, maybe equally excited. She even informed him not to pick Kalsha up until tomorrow morning. Not that he'd be spending the night however it would be late and Sadie, Mac and Kalsha would be sleeping. Back to spending the night. He'd love to, only it was too soon. He'd have to wait. He wasn't sure how long but no matter how much he wanted to, he wouldn't be spending the night with Shana tonight.

* * * *

Kal parked his car and practically bounded up the steps to Shana's apartment. He knocked. The door opened and Shana smiled at him. Her face lit up when she smiled. It was such a beautiful smile, with beautiful full lips waiting to be kissed. And he almost did kiss them. Then she turned back into her apartment to grab a sweater and her purse. Damn, but he wanted to kiss her. He walked slowly down the steps behind her. When they reached the Vet, he opened the door for her and she got in. From this vantage point, he had a great view of her cleavage. Hell, he wanted to do more than kiss her lips. He wanted to have his hands and lips all over her breasts. Just how long did he have to wait anyway? Kal got in and turned to Shana.

"Ready?" Kal asked.

"Yes," Shana said turning towards him.

Kal couldn't help himself as he leaned toward her, cupping her chin and helping himself to those full ripe lips—lips eagerly responding to his need. He broke the kiss and cleared his throat. "I've been waiting all day to do that," he said, smiling his sexy smile.

"Me, too," Shana said, surprising herself and him.

"Let's go grab a burger," Kal said and drove slowly out of the parking lot. He was relieved with her response, although she was quiet now. But then again it was hard to talk with all the noise and wind from having the top down. So he turned up the stereo. He had Mick Sterling, a Minneapolis Blues singer, playing. "Is this music okay?"

"Yes. I have this CD. It's one of my favorites."

"Mine, too," Kal said smiling.

"But you have to be from Minnesota to appreciate it, I suppose."

"Right. People down here don't have a clue who Mick is," Kal said laughing as he pulled into Mel's Diner.

After being seated, Kal ordered burgers, fries and Cokes for both of them.

"I can't believe you like Mick?" Shana said.

"I used to listen to him play at Bunkers in downtown Minneapolis."

"Me, too."

"I think I have all his CDs, too. And they are well used."

"I have three of his."

"We'll have to compare CDs, you may want to borrow one of mine."

"I wonder if they have any good local Blues bands in Phoenix?"

"Sad to admit, but I haven't actually checked it out since I moved here. However I'd be game to listen to some local bands and see if we can find any as good as Mick."

"I'd be open to that."

Taking Chances

"How about next Friday night? We can pick up the latest issue of the *Phoenix Night Scene* weekly paper and pick a band to try."

"Okay," Shana said.

The burgers came. They were greasy on toasted buns. The only way to eat burgers! Crinkle cut fries and Coke in the old-fashioned Coke glasses. "Um! These are good!" Shana said.

"I've checked out numerous places and Mel's is the best burger place I've found," Kal said and had to stop himself because he'd almost said it was Kalsha's favorite, too.

"What movie are we going to?"

"You said you like action and romance, so there is a new James Bond movie out, that should be both."

"Great! I love James Bond. Pierce Brosnan is my favorite."

"There is a new James Bond, you know."

"Yes, not sure I like that, although I'm willing to give him a shot."

"Okay. Bond it is," Kal said as he took out a twenty for the check.

* * * *

Since there was time before the movie started, they took the slow route to the movie theater via Old Scottsdale. Kal pointed out places of interest while they both sang along to Mick cranked on the stereo. They arrived promptly at the movie theater fifteen minutes prior to the start time.

They stood gazing at the snack menu hanging behind the concession stand, after getting their tickets.

"Medium popcorn and two Cokes?" Kal asked Shana.

"Yes," she answered.

Kal nodded and the clerk poured their Cokes and bagged their popcorn.

As they took their seats and got comfortable for the movie, Shana tried to remember the last time she'd been to a movie theater. She couldn't. It'd been a long time. She'd been alone a long time, and when you're alone you don't go to movies; you simply wait and rent the DVD. It felt good to be at an actual movie theater, with a man, on a date. She was actually enjoying herself. She smiled at Kal. He smiled back, however before she could say anything, the previews started, so she leaned back and settled into her comfy reclining chair, next to her date.

Three hours later, they watched the credits scroll by.

"So, what'd you think? Like the new James Bond?" Kal asked.

"I wasn't so sure I would, but I did!"

"Great action scenes," Kal said.

"Great romance scenes!" Shana said laughing.

"Touché!" Kal said joining her laughter as they exited the theater.

A deep blue sky filled with sparkling stars and a lower much more comfortable temperature greeted them.

"What a gorgeous night," Kal said as they got in the Vet.

"Yes. It seems Arizona has many of them." And gorgeous men she thought. She wanted one for herself. She was beginning to think Kal would do very nicely.

* * * *

They talked and laughed as they drove to her apartment. Kal parked and looked into Shana's eyes. He didn't want to say good-bye yet although it was almost one in the morning. He wanted her too much to even think about walking her to her door. It would be dangerous. He wasn't sure he could stop at the door. If he went in, things could get out of hand quickly and despite his prior misgivings, he liked her. He didn't want to screw up their chance at a relationship. And a lot depended on how their dating progressed.

Kal parked at the end of the parking lot in an end spot next to a palm tree. It was a habit of his when he drove the Vet. He didn't want to take any chances with door dings. He got out, walked around to her door and opened it. Shana got out, he closed the door and the next minute he had her back against the car with his arms around her, kissing her. It was a hungry-devouring kiss and she was giving it back with an equal amount of hunger. Her arms wrapped around his neck. Kal swung them around so he was leaning on the car. His hands slid down to her waist and then her sweet ass. He pulled her to him pressing his groin into her, so she would know what she did to him. He kissed her neck and eased one hand up to her breast cupping it. He heard her moan.

Taking Chances

"Do you want to come up to my apartment?"

"Can't," Kal moaned in between kisses.

"Why?" Shana asked.

"I promised you slow," Kal barely got out.

"Oh, is this slow?" Shana teased and leaning back looked into his handsome face.

"Yes, this is slow," Kal gritted out like he was in pain. "I'm trying to keep my promise, but woman, you turn me on!"

"Yes. Slow," Shana stated.

"I want you, Shana. I want to have a relationship with you. What do you want?" Kal kissed her neck again and pressed his groin into her heat.

"I want ... to go slow," Shana said.

"Do you want me?"

Her body was on fire. Hell, yes she wanted him. She'd have to be dead to not want him. She'd been *almost dead* for too long. But she wasn't now. She was alive and yes, she wanted him. "Yes," she whispered.

"How long do we have to wait?" He kissed her ear, then her cheek.

"We-need-to-go-on-six-dates," Shana got out slowly, one word at a time.

"What number is this?" Kal asked, thinking six was a doable number. Maybe.

"What ... Oh. Date three." She couldn't concentrate with his slow, sensual attack on her senses.

"Three to go then," Kal managed to get out. He stood up holding her in front of him. "Would you like to go golfing tomorrow morning?"

"Sure. What time?"

"Eight and we'll have brunch after we're done at the Club House restaurant."

"Okay," Shana said and leaned up and kissed him. "Tomorrow." She turned and walked across the parking lot towards her apartment, a huge smile played across her face.

Kal leaned back against his car and watched her hips sway provocatively as she walked. Yes, tomorrow. And that would be

101

number four. And that left only two more. He could make it until then with the help of a few cold showers.

Chapter Eleven

Shana lay in bed thinking about her date. About Kal. She could still feel his kisses and when she closed her eyes, she could see him smiling and pressing his body against hers. The visions in her mind of lying in bed with him were still vivid from their first meeting. Yes, she'd drunk too much that night, however she remembered every minute of their sexual encounter. After they finished, she fell asleep and was out for the night, still she remembered everything up until then. It had been damn good. Their attraction was strong then and it hadn't dimmed at all. No, it was as strong as ever. It would be good again. She just had to forget about what happened. She hadn't had a choice. Not really. Maybe she didn't have to tell him. Women terminated pregnancies every day and the men never found out about it. Not unless the women actually told them. She was not going to think about it now. No, she was going to go to sleep dreaming about making mad passionate love with Kal.

* * * *

Bright streaks of sun shone through the cracks in the blinds on Shana's bedroom window. She woke up with a smile on her face. She would be seeing Kal again. Lazily she turned to look at the clock and she practically jumped out of bed. She only had an hour before he arrived. The alarm must've gone off and she'd hit the snooze button, again. Damn!

A short time later, Shana stood on the first tee of Scottsdale Hills golf course. There was a gentle breeze and the sun shone brightly. As usual. She was nervous; it had been quite a few years ago since she last played golf. If she could just talk herself through the first tee and manage a decent swing, she would probably do okay. It was when she stopped to think about every minute part of her swing that she had problems. Shana stared at the flag in the hole, then the ball on the tee. She held her breath and took her swing. Her eyes followed the ball as it went up and fell midway to the hole.

"Good shot, Shana," Kal said.

"Thanks." Shana walked back to the golf cart. She stopped and turned to watch Kal's swing. It looked good. He looked real good, too. She watched the ball land gently on the green. "Very nice," she said to Kal as he walked back towards her. He stopped in front of her and gave her a light quick kiss on the cheek.

The morning went quickly and before she knew it, they finished golfing nine holes and headed inside the clubhouse for brunch. They were seated outside on the patio with a gorgeous view of the lush green golf course sprinkled with cactus and palm trees.

"Let's get some food." Kal got up and walked towards the buffet and Shana followed. "They have a great brunch here. You'll have to try the caramel rolls. They bake them here so they are always fresh."

"I love caramel rolls, especially fresh ones!" Shana said.

Kal kept the conversation light while they ate. They sipped mimosas slowly and watched the golfers go by in their golf carts.

"You played a nice game of golf," Kal said.

"I think I got lucky today. Probably because it's been so long since I last golfed."

"Maybe you're just a good golfer," Kal said, teasing.

"We'll see if my luck holds out after I golf a few more times."

"You could join a ladies golf league."

"It'd probably be better for my ego to golf with women, but then again some women are as good as the men."

"True. What counts is if you enjoy the day golfing, not what your score is."

"Either way I had a great day. I enjoyed the day and I am thrilled with my score. How about you?" Shana asked.

"I am thoroughly enjoying my day, and my score is always good, so I can't complain. And I have no complaints about my golf partner."

Taking Chances

"Thanks," Shana said blushing a little. "Why did you move to Phoenix? For year round golfing?" she asked changing the subject.

"I, like you, enjoy the sun. I love Minnesota. Don't get me wrong, but it gets damn cold in the winter."

"I know. Winters are tough there."

"Don't you have family back in Minnesota?"

"No. My parents were killed in a car accident when I was in college. My sister, Sadie lives here."

"So that's why you came here then?"

* * * *

"That and the sun," Kal laughed. He felt uneasy mentioning Sadie even though that didn't mean the subject of Kalsha would be brought up. Not yet anyway.

"It's going to feel strange spending Thanksgiving and Christmas here without cold weather and snow."

"It does feel different, but you get used to it." Kal's thoughts drifted to spending the holidays with Shana. When he thought about it, he felt excited and full of anticipation. Unfortunately, they had a huge obstacle to get over before that could ever happen. The server brought the check, Kal handed her a Visa card and she walked away. "Any plans for the rest of the day?" he said to Shana.

"Just some errands to run."

Kal signed the credit card receipt for the server and they headed to the parking lot. He walked up beside her and gently put his arm around her waist. When they reached the Vet, he took her in his arms and kissed her.

"Very nice," Shana whispered.

"My sentiments exactly. We should do this more often." And he kissed her again lightly, released her slowly and opened her door. "But not in the golf club house parking lot."

Shana giggled and got in. "You're right."

Kal took the long way back, cruising slowly down Scottsdale Road to Shana's apartment. After parking, he walked her to her door. Stopping in front of the door, he took her in his arms and stared into her beautiful eyes. "I like having you in my arms. I like you."

"I like you, too, Kal."

"Any plans for tomorrow night?" Kal asked.

"Not yet, why do you ask?"

"It's Monday Night Football and the Vikings are playing. There's this great sports bar, The End Zone, over by the hospital, where I usually watch the game. Care to join me?"

"The Vikings, huh. Well, no true Minnesotan could turn that down. Whether they liked football or not."

"Do you like football?" Kal asked a little worried she might hate football.

"Only if the Vikings are playing," she teased.

"It's a date then?"

"Wouldn't miss it."

"Great! Date five it is. Meet me in the parking lot after work tomorrow."

"Okay." Shana leaned up to receive his kiss.

Kal walked to the car feeling absolutely ecstatic. He felt like he was in high school experiencing his first real crush on a girl. He could tell her barriers were coming down. The crescendo of their relationship was building along with his sexual frustrations. Saturday night would be the big night, although he was looking forward to Monday night, too.

* * * *

Kal drove straight to Sadie's to pick up Kalsha. The rest of the day was for Kalsha. Her smiling little face always lit up his days. Only now, every time he looked at Kalsha, he saw Shana's face.

Kal pulled up in the driveway, parked, and walked in after a polite quick knock on the front door. He was anxious to see Kalsha and didn't wait for Sadie to come to the door.

"So, how was your date?" Sadie asked, as Kal walked in.

"Dates," Kal corrected.

"Oh. Did you ..." Sadie started to ask.

"No. We went out to a movie last night. And we played golf and had brunch today."

Taking Chances

"And in between that time?" Sadie prompted looking for more details.

"I went home alone."

"Good. Wouldn't want you two moving too fast now would we?"

"I promised slow," Kal stated.

"And that means what? A week?"

"Yeah, about a week."

"Are you sure about this?"

"I like her more every time I see her. So we decided on six dates before we even think about having sex."

"Really. And what date are you on?"

"Tomorrow night will be five."

"Moving quickly, I see. Obviously, you are in a hurry to get to number six. But a date on Monday night?" Sadie queried.

"Monday Night Football," Kal responded matter-of-factly, as if she should have guessed that.

"The Vikings are playing, I got it."

"So can you watch Kalsha tomorrow night?" Kal asked, smiling.

"What if we had plans?"

"I knew your plans would be in your theater room watching the Vikings on your big screen television."

"What can I say?" Sadie questioned.

"Yes?"

"Of course. Kalsha can watch the game with me and Mac."

"Thanks, Sis," Kal said hugging her. "You're the best."

* * * *

Shana spent the night checking out the Vikings players and the team stats. Heck, she didn't want to be clueless about what was going on now, did she? Probably wouldn't be a lot of Vikings fans at the bar though. She dug through her box of winter clothes and found her Vikings shirt. She'd bought one a few years ago when she'd won tickets at work to a Vikings game. That was the only time she'd ever worn it. Today she was very glad she'd kept it.

* * * *

Rose Marie Meuwissen

After work, Shana changed into jeans and her Vikings shirt. She grabbed her light jacket and went to meet Kal in the parking lot. To her amazement, she spotted Kal next to his Vet and he was wearing a Vikings T-shirt also. "Well, don't we look like a couple of Minnesotans," she said walking up to him.

"Nice shirt," he said realizing she must've brought it from Minnesota. Good. He was a big Vikings fan and he was happy to see she was also a fan.

"You, too!" Shana said.

"Hop in," Kal said opening the door. "We'll come back for your car after the game because parking will be tough at the bar."

Shana couldn't imagine why, but to her amazement when they arrived, the parking lot was almost full. She was shocked when they walked into a standing room only bar swathed in purple shirts. "I never expected to see so many Vikings fans in Phoenix!"

"Most of these fans hale from Minnesota," Kal said.

"I guess I hadn't thought about that," she said scanning the room for empty seats as she followed Kal through the fans to the back of the bar where they were greeted by two other couples in purple Vikings shirts.

"This is, Shana," Kal said to the other couples. "Shana, this is Tom and Susie and Fred and Bonnie. They're from Minnesota and huge Vikings fans."

"Hi, Shana," they each said separately.

"Hi, nice to meet all of you," Shana replied and took a seat on a stool next to Kal at the table. She watched the pre-game festivities on the large screen. A monstrous Viking ship appeared in the Metrodome and the players ran out to the field. The dome was filled to capacity with cheering fans. However, it was the familiar site of the Metrodome, and downtown Minneapolis, that evoked the memories of home. She was overwhelmed by her feelings. The sound level in the bar was high. A few minutes later, she turned back towards Kal to find him staring at her.

"Everything okay?" Kal asked with a concerned look on his face.

"Yes, just felt a little homesick seeing the Metrodome."

Taking Chances

"Watching the Vikings play always makes me think about Minnesota," Kal stated.

"That makes me feel better," Shana said, feeling reassured she wasn't the only one.

"In fact, that's probably why all these people are here today. They're from Minnesota and it's a way to still feel Minnesotan and support the home team with fellow Minnesotans."

"I think I'm going to like watching the Vikings play this season," she said thoughtfully and smiled at Kal. Then to her surprise he leaned forward, wrapped his arms around her and kissed her lips, just as the Vikings scored a touchdown.

* * * *

Kal dropped Shana off back at her car in the hospital parking lot. It was getting late and they had to work in the morning so he knew they had to get going. But he turned her in his arms for one last kiss for the evening, before he said goodbye.

"I had a very nice time. Thanks for taking me," Shana said after the kiss ended and she looked up into his handsome tanned face.

"The pleasure was all mine," Kal said, nibbling and kissing her neck.

"I really should get going." He was turning her on, yet she was determined to wait.

"Shana, every time I see you, the more I like you. You are so beautiful. You're great company and I know I could fall in love with you." Kal pressed his lips gently on hers. He held her tightly as he felt her body sway slightly.

"Kal, I don't know what to say. I like you. I like you a lot."

"I'd like to take you to Lake Havasu this weekend."

"Overnight?"

"Yes, but we won't do anything you don't feel comfortable with. It'll be up to you."

"Okay," she said without any hesitation.

"Saturday morning then. I'll pick you up at eight." Kal released her to open her car door, so she could get in. Shana got in and closed the door. She started the engine and put the driver's window down. Kal leaned down and reached in to tip her chin up for one last kiss. "Till Saturday," he said, stood up, turned and walked back to his car.

Shana forced herself to breathe. Her heart was pounding in her chest, even though she smiled as she watched him walk away. Breathe, she thought, just breathe. She was giddy, so giddy she had to pinch her arm. Yes, she was awake and no, this wasn't a dream. This was real.

* * * *

Shana could hardly believe it was Friday already. The week had sped by so quickly. She'd only talked briefly with Kal in the halls of the hospital when passing. Today, she received an email from Kal saying he was out golfing and wouldn't be in this afternoon, however would be at her house bright and early at eight on Saturday morning.

She needed to pack a bag for the weekend. It had been a long time since she'd spent the night with a man. And what a coincidence the last time she had was with Kal over two years ago. She felt a small stab of guilt about it. Although she was a grown woman and it was her choice to make. Would her mother approve? Probably not, but then she would never know. This time she was on the pill so there would be no accidents. She wanted to lie naked next to Kal in bed and be able to let her hands freely roam over his body. And she longed to feel his strong hands roam gently over her body. In fact, that part excited her the most. Not that the actual sexual intercourse wouldn't be fantastic. Oh heck, she wanted it all, and she wouldn't have long to wait. Only hours now.

Shana hit the alarm's off button at six thirty. Once she finally got her mind to stop racing, she'd slept hard. Standing in the shower, the hot water rolling over her body, the radio playing *Slow Hand* by the Pointer Sisters, Shana couldn't help but sing along. She was happy. Finally. It had been too long. Way too long. And this could end up being the best time of her life.

* * * *

"Bye, Baby. Love you," Kal said hugging and kissing Kalsha. "Daddy will be back to pick you up tomorrow night." Kalsha was hugging his neck fiercely and kissing his cheek.

"Love Daddy," Kalsha said.

Taking Chances

Kal set her down and walked to the door to leave. "I really appreciate this, Sadie."

"I consider it an investment in the future," Sadie said smiling at Kal.

"Investment in what?" Kal asked not following her train of thought.

"A mother for Kalsha," Sadie answered.

"And you thought I was moving fast?" Kal questioned.

"I'm not trying to rush you. Take your time and see what happens."

"I will. I like her. It all depends if we can both get past what happened before."

"Forgiveness is a huge step, and it can give peace to everyone involved," Sadie said, her eyes full of hope. "That's enough of my lecturing, get out of here and have a great weekend!"

"I'm going," Kal said as Sadie shooed him out the door.

* * * *

His expectations were high for their weekend together. He reserved a room at the London Bridge Resort on Lake Havasu with a view of the lake. His sleep the night before had been filled with dreams of making love to Shana. He still remembered her sexy body. Tan and trim lying beneath him. Her blond hair fanned out on the pillow. Her eyes glazed with passion as her body arched to meet his. Damn! He had to stop thinking about it. He'd woke with a hard on, and now he was hard again. Better change his train of thought so he could get out of the car without embarrassing himself.

The top was down on the Vet and the wind blew wildly around his face. The sun was just rising behind the Superstition Mountains. He pulled into her parking lot and eagerly got out of the Vet. He couldn't wait to see Shana.

* * * *

Shana watched the Vet pull into the parking lot. He looked so good. So handsome. Tonight could not get here soon enough. She wanted to kiss him and not stop anytime soon. One last quick look in the mirror and she walked to the door as he knocked. She opened the door. "Hi," she said smiling brightly up at Kal.

"Hi," Kal said huskily as he pulled her into his arms. "I've been waiting all night to do this." He eagerly joined their lips with a kiss that promised the passion to come. Then he released her, searching her eyes for signs of her reaction and thoughts.

"I'm ready," Shana said. She reached for her bag, which Kal promptly took from her hand.

"I'll carry that," he said smiling.

Shana put her hair up in a clip and they took off for their weekend adventure. Soon they were on the freeway heading north to Lake Havasu with the stereo blasting out Mick's raspy voice. A couple of hours later they arrived in Lake Havasu. She'd googled Lake Havasu on the internet so she would know what to expect. It was a small town on the lake in northern Arizona, probably much like the small lake towns in northern Minnesota. Probably full of Minnesota snowbirds. She figured she would like it and as soon as they arrived at the lake, she knew she liked it. Most likely because it reminded her of northern Minnesota. It felt like home. She hadn't realized how much she'd missed home until now.

"I think I'm going to like this town," she said eyeing the lake, as he pulled into the parking lot of a hotel right on the lake.

"I thought you would. Always reminds me of Minnesota."

"Where are we staying?" Shana asked hoping it was this hotel.

"Here at the London Bridge Resort. We should have a view of the lake," Kal said.

"Very nice," Shana said, looking at the beautiful lake front resort.

"Let's check in and then we can take a walk and check out the area," Kal said turning the car off and getting out.

The room was fabulous, decorated in English floral patterns, English provincial furniture, and a patio facing the lake. One bed. One king size bed. She eyed the bed thoughtfully. She could see herself and Kal on the bed making love. Love? Had she just thought that? Probably not love, yet, though she was getting there quickly.

"Do you like it?" Kal asked.

"I couldn't ask for anything more."

Taking Chances

"Are you okay with the one bed?" Kal asked, suddenly concerned by the look on her face.

"Yes."

"Great!" Kal walked up to her and wrapped his arms around her. He gently kissed her lips. Short and sweet, nothing more. He needed to go slow tonight so as not to scare her. He gently took her hand and they left the room to go exploring. They walked outside to the sidewalk pathway alongside the lake.

"This is the London Bridge," Kal said looking up at the bridge spanning Lake Havasu.

"As in the song 'London Bridge is Falling Down'?" Shana asked scanning the bridge with her eyes.

"Not sure about that, but possibly."

"Is it actually from London?"

"Yes, it is the original London Bridge. It was dismantled piece by piece. Every piece was numbered so they could put it back together exactly right," Kal explained.

"Oh," Shana said staring intently at the bridge. "It's a very visually appealing bridge, but I thought the London Bridge was much bigger and ornate."

"Very good," Kal teased. "Actually, the one you are probably thinking about is the Tower Bridge which everyone thinks mistakenly is the London Bridge."

"Yes, I remember towers. So this is a different bridge then."

"Right. The story goes that the people, who sold the town of Lake Havasu the bridge, didn't explain that to the town at the time of the sale. And the town of Lake Havasu thought they were getting the other bridge," Kal explained.

"That doesn't make any sense. Didn't they see a picture of it or go over and look at it before buying it?" Shana asked out of frustration for the town.

"Not sure, but like I said it is hearsay, and I think the town of Lake Havasu is happy to have it now. It's an excellent tourist attraction for them and draws thousands of visitors to the area each year," Kal said as they continued walking along the shore.

"Want to grab some lunch?" Kal asked.

"Yes, I'm starving," she replied and laughed.

"Have you ever been to In N Out Burger?"

"No. Are they good?"

"Everything they have is fresh-the burgers, fries and malts made the old fashioned way."

"Let's go! I'm starving and you're making me hungrier talking about it." She grabbed his hand. "Lead on."

They walked up the hill toward the main street to the In N Out Burger and ordered.

"This is good. Really good," Shana said, enjoying every bite.

"So you like it, huh?"

"Wasn't sure if it would be good. Seeing it is a fast food chain. But it is," Shana said, finishing her burger, fries and Coke.

"Glad you like it."

The afternoon passed quickly as they browsed the shops looking at all the tourist items for the London Bridge. Shana bought a small replica souvenir of the bridge. They stopped at the ice cream shop and each ordered an ice cream cone which they leisurely ate sitting on the stone wall along the lake's walkway on the shoreline.

After four, they headed up to their hotel room to relax for a while and change for dinner. To say it felt a little awkward was an understatement. She was in a hotel room with a man. Kal must've sensed her unease, so he went down to the gift shop to pick up some Cokes and bottled water for later, after he showered and dressed. This allowed her time to change and get ready alone. What a nice guy!

After freshening up, she slipped on a short, teal spaghetti strapped sundress and touched up her makeup and hair. Shana just sat down on the bed to slip her sandals on when the door opened. He'd been gone over thirty minutes, so she knew he'd done it to give her time to get ready.

"Wow, you look great!" Kal said setting the bottles on the table, not taking his eyes off her.

"Thanks," Shana said as she walked towards Kal.

Kal's hand slipped under her chin and he kissed her gently at first, then with more intensity as he drew her body against him. Ending the kiss he said, "Just wanted to wet your appetite for later."

Taking Chances

Shana regained her composure after nearly melting in his arms. "I'll be counting the minutes," she said looking him in the eyes so he could see the raw passion smoldering in them.

Kal cleared his voice. "With that said, we'd better go have dinner before we no longer find ourselves interested in dinner at all."

"I'm looking forward to dinner, and I'm looking forward to what comes after dinner, too."

Kal grinned. "Touché'," he said and followed her out the door.

Their reservation was at the London Bridge Resort's own Martini Bay Restaurant. It was a beautiful night, clear skies and still warm. Kal had reserved a table outside on the patio with a view of the lake.

"This is lovely," Shana said after they were seated.

"Yes, it is," Kal said. "However my date is far more lovely. She is truly captivating."

Shana actually blushed at that remark. The waiter appeared with their glasses of wine. Knowing it was a Martini Bar, she opted to try a martini after dinner instead of before, since she was not sure if it would be a good choice on an empty stomach. Both opted for one of the pasta seafood specials. They sat quietly and watched the boats on the lake coming in for the night to dock. It almost resembled a floating red and green light display in the evening light.

"So, how did you like your day so far?" Kal asked.

"I have loved every minute of it. You are a great guide."

"Thank you, Madame," Kal said jokingly. "Hope the rest of the night meets your expectations, also."

The wild sexy look on his face almost did her in. This was almost like being a part of a romance novel love story. Boy meets girl, they fall in love and live happily ever after. "I'm sure it will," she managed to say. Thankfully, the food was served only minutes later.

They ate and discussed the charm of the quaint little town of Lake Havasu. The martinis were ordered in lieu of dessert. Shana ordered a chocolate one hoping it would taste like chocolate, since she actually didn't like the taste of hard liquor.

"How is your martini?" Kal asked as he watched her try her first sip.

"Tastes like chocolate. Sort of anyway. Doesn't actually taste like liquor."

"I'm assuming that's good?"

"Yes. Because then I may be able to drink it." She only managed to drink about half before they left.

The sun had set and lights now adorned the bridge and its surroundings, casting a golden hue on the area. They strolled along the railing of the hotel's veranda, hand in hand. Mellow, easy listening music played through the hotel's scattered outside speakers. Kal stood behind her at the railing with his arms around her waist and his lips against her hair.

"I enjoyed our day together. I really like being with you," he said turning her into his arms. He gently brushed aside the windblown hair from her face and kissed her. "Are you ready to go upstairs?" he asked.

"Yes, I'm ready, Kal."

* * * *

In the room, Kal poured them each a Coke over ice. He joined Shana on the patio with their glasses of Coke. She was standing at the railing deep in thought waiting for him. He stood next to her and handed her a glass. "Over the last weeks, it's proven extremely difficult to leave you after each date. I want to spend even more time with you. And the thought of not having to leave you tonight is thoroughly exhilarating."

"Me, too." Shana turned towards Kal. She set her glass down, leaned into him and gently brushed her lips over his. "Me, too."

Kal set his glass down quickly and took her in his arms. He kissed her with all the passion and emotions he'd kept bottled up inside all these weeks. His mouth moved to her ear, her neck and then her shoulder. He pressed her body against his with his hands pressed against her butt. His one hand slid lower to her bare thigh below the hem of her dress. Smooth firm skin greeted him and as he moved upward under her dress, he felt her bare butt framed in a string thong. He was rock hard and it would take all the willpower he had left to move slowly.

Taking Chances

He pulled back from her to guide her inside, closing the patio door behind him. He sat on the edge of the bed pulling her onto his lap. He took her face in his hands and began kissing her again. The strap of her dress slid down to rest on her arm as his kiss moved down her chest, to the ridge where skin met dress. Her breasts threatened to escape their confines. His hand roamed the bare skin of her thigh where her dress had slid up and was now riding at her hip. His other hand found the zipper on her dress, eased it down, and allowed the front to fall revealing her breasts riding high in a skimpy push up bra.

His eyes fixated on the lush fevered skin as his hand moved from thigh to breast. He swiftly unhooked the bra and watched it slide forward and down. He cupped her breast. He heard her moan softly with pleasure. She leaned into him, her hands caressing his face and hair. Quickly, he eased the dress over her head taking the bra along with it.

He lifted her to the center of the turned down bed while their lips were still hungrily locked together. He heard the clunk of her shoes hitting the floor as she slipped them off. She began unbuttoning his shirt, while he undid his belt and pants. Quickly he stood up and shed his shirt, pants and shoes. With only his boxers left he looked into her watching and waiting eyes. Waiting for him. At that moment, he knew she wanted this as much as he did.

He dropped the boxers and slid into the bed next to her. Immediately he took her in his arms and pressed his passion-filled lips against her soft and yielding lips, as his hand kneaded her breast. His lips closely followed his hand to her breast. His hand slowly moved from her breast to the thong, sliding it down her legs to free her. No more barriers. She was his now. His searching hand found her wet and he slid his finger into her heat as she arched to meet his thrust.

"Now," she said. She couldn't take anymore, she wanted him inside her. Her body arched wildly against him.

"Do I need a condom?" he asked, barely holding back. "Or are you on the pill?"

"I'm on the pill," she gasped and immediately she felt his rock hard erection enter her body. Her body writhed in pleasure and she climaxed shortly after penetration. She felt his climax only seconds later.

He kissed her lips and rolled to her side completely sated. His hand gently caressed her stomach. "That was great." *A little quick but it'd been a long time.*

"Yes, it was," she said smiling.

"We should do this more often," Kal suggested.

"More than once every couple years?"

"More like every day," he countered. "And all night long."

"That could be a possibility," Shana said as she slowly drifted off to sleep, her body entirely relaxed.

Kal reached down, pulled the sheet over them, pulled her body up against his, and holding her tight fell asleep.

* * * *

Kal woke when the sun was rising. He looked over at Shana still asleep. She was a beautiful, sexy woman. She was the mother of his child. And she was the woman he was in love with. They had some major talking to do before they could move to the next step. However she was here now, naked in his bed, and he was going to make love to her again before they left. And he was going to start right now.

Chapter Twelve

After spending the weekend together, it was difficult to go home. Her body had been reawakened to the pleasures of lovemaking, which were highly addictive. She could not be satisfied with just one taste without wanting more. All she could think of was making love to Kal again. She'd never felt such a strong bond with anyone before. It was difficult to describe, however she knew she felt a high comfort level in being with Kal. It simply felt natural and uncontrived. He'd emailed her at work and called every night. Her anticipation of his calls was intense. It was already Friday and they were going out to dinner and, hopefully, he would be spending the night with her. She was ready and watching out the window for his car to pull up. She grabbed her purse and sweater and ran down to the car as soon as he arrived.

"Hi, Beautiful!" Kal said as she walked up to the car.

Shana saw the pleased expression on his face, and knew she'd selected the right clothes; skin tight jean capris and a body hugging black tank top. As she bent down to get into the car, she noted his eyes riveted on her breasts. She was just as attracted to him and the idea of skipping dinner and running upstairs to her apartment, into her bedroom where they would make passionate love tempted her. She knew she would have to wait, so instead, she stood on tiptoe and kissed him fully on the lips, her body flush against his. The kiss deepened as she felt the flames igniting. Her body was responding with rising passion.

Kal broke the kiss and whispered in her ear, "This will have to wait."

"I know," she answered reluctantly.

"So what are you hungry for?" Kal asked.

Shana couldn't help smiling. "I'm assuming you mean, besides you."

"Hey, we can skip eating and head right up those stairs to your place."

"I am hungry," Shana said. "For food, I mean."

"So, how about we do both."

Shana looked confused. "How?" she asked.

"We can go back up to your place and order pizza a little later," Kal suggested with a wicked grin as his hand roamed her jean-clad thigh.

Shana teased, "Talked me into it."

Kal turned off the car and they got out. Within minutes, he was by her side with his arm around her waist and they were running to the apartment.

She pulled her keys out and opened the door. They quickly entered with Kal closing the door behind them. They were on fire for each other. Kal pulled Shana into his arms and kissed her lips fast and hard. He pressed her body against his as he leaned against the closed door. His hand slid under her tank top as her fingers deftly unbuttoned his shirt. He pulled her top up over her head. She pulled at his now unbuttoned shirt, deftly moving it up and out of his jeans. He finished for her and it was now on the floor along with her shirt. Her black, sexy push-bra caused her breasts to thrust forward, pressing against his bare chest. Quickly his fingers managed to unhook her bra, freeing her mounds of flesh, now his for the taking. His mouth moved to her breast and she moaned.

Their passions had risen quickly and heat engulfed them. Her hand was reaching for his manhood, now cupping him over his jeans. Eagerly and quickly, her capris and his jeans along with underwear joined the pile on the floor. His hands pulled her legs up and she wrapped them around his waist. He braced his hands under her butt and carried her to the couch, sitting down with Shana still straddling him. Their lips remained locked and Shana raised her body up placing her breasts now in reach of Kal's lips. He eagerly caught one and sucked the ripe taut nipple aggressively. He was rock hard and pushing up against her opening. His patience had quickly reached its limit and he released his mouth from her breast, moving her down swiftly, onto his hard shaft. Seeking and finding her lips again with fierce hunger, he devoured her mouth. Shana rode him fast and deep with them both climaxing within moments of each other. Their hearts were still pounding as they collapsed against each other.

"Unbelievable," Kal whispered against Shana's cheek.

"Can't say I've ever experienced anything like that before."

"That's good, right?" he asked.

Shana detected worry in his voice that she perhaps hadn't enjoyed it. She replied, "Very good," leaned forward and kissed his lips.

Kal grinned and kissed her back. "So are you still hungry?"

"Yes, but for food this time," she answered.

"Do you still want to go out to eat?"

"How about we order that pizza you mentioned earlier, and then we can watch a movie?"

"Works for me," Kal answered.

After getting dressed, Shana called and ordered the pizza. They decided to watch a chic flick, as Kal called it, *Because I Said So*, and because she only had chic flicks.

"We can watch TV until the pizza gets here," she offered turning it on.

The pizza arrived thirty minutes later, and they spread it out on the coffee table, sat on the floor and ate. Shana put the movie in after they finished eating and had cleaned up. Kal and Shana moved to the couch. He pulled her close wrapping his arms around her while they watched the movie and laughed together.

The movie ended and Kal and Shana were lying side by side on the couch. Shana had enjoyed how he'd caressed her body during the entire movie, pleased he couldn't keep his hands off her.

* * * *

Kal felt drawn to her with every fiber of his being. The attraction remained strong even though they had just satisfied their sexual desire a few hours earlier. He wanted her again and he was confident she was feeling the same intense attraction. At least he thought she was until she abruptly stood up. She turned toward him and held out her hand to him.

Kal stood up not knowing what she wanted, so he took her in his arms and kissed her. She kissed him back and then broke off the kiss, taking his hand and leading him to the bedroom.

She pulled the comforter down on the bed to open the sheets for them. She had him wondering if she wanted him to spend the night, for why else would she be turning down the bedding? For Shana, Kal guessed this was a big step to have him spend the night. It was almost like they knew what the other was thinking because they both started peeling off their clothes quickly. Kal finished first and helped Shana finish, then pulled her down on the bed on top of him. This time they made love slowly, touching every inch of each other's body with both lips and hands. After a sweet release for both, Shana put her head on Kal's chest and relaxed, closing her eyes.

Kal was fully relaxed and almost asleep, also. He kissed her hair lightly, breathing in her fragrance, caressing her bare back gently. He was in love with her. He wasn't sure before however now he knew for sure.

"I love you, Shana," he said softly. He felt safe saying it out loud because he knew she was sleeping. He wasn't however so sure about what he was going to do about it. They needed to talk. No, they had to talk to move forward in their relationship. It wasn't going to be fun. No, not at all. It was going to be one of the most difficult conversations of his life. Keeping the truth about that night was wearing heavily on his conscience. Hopefully, when he got up the courage to tell her, the conversation would have a good ending. He wanted her to meet Kalsha. He felt sure she would immediately fall in love with Kalsha. Kalsha was truly a gift from God. He would have to make a decision. Decide when to have this talk. Maybe he should tell her he loved her first. When she was awake, of course. Yes, that's what he'd do. With that Kal fell asleep holding Shana tightly to him.

* * * *

Shana felt it in his breathing when Kal fell asleep. She'd just about drifted off completely when she felt his hands caressing her back. It felt wonderful and she was just about to fall asleep when she could hardly

Taking Chances

believe her ears. She'd heard Kal say he loved her. She didn't know how to respond so she pretended to be asleep. And it had worked because he hadn't said anything else. Her heart felt heavy knowing she had to tell him what she'd done. And she needed to do it soon, before she got any more involved with Kal. Because she didn't know what he would do after he found out. She could easily lose him again. It could get downright nasty. Right now, she felt good. Way, too, good to spoil her mood by thinking about it. In fact, she was going to forget about it right now and go to sleep. She felt so good lying in his arms. He had since rolled to his side enfolding her in his arms or as they call it—spooning. Within minutes, she was asleep.

Shana was still half-asleep when she felt her body being caressed ever so gently. It took a minute to clear her mind to remember Kal was lying next to her. And it was he that lovingly caressed her. She was enjoying it immensely so she lay still a while longer. When she could take no more, because her body was primed and ready, she turned into his arms to face him so she could kiss his lips. His lips met hers eagerly and he pulled her tightly against him.

* * * *

Kal was ready. He'd been ready for a long time. His hands roamed freely over her silky skin, over the soft breast filling his hand. He knew he should've waited until she woke up, but it had been such a long time since he'd spent the night with a woman, except for the weekend trip to Lake Havasu with Shana and he was enjoying himself greatly. He hadn't dated much at all with having to take care of Kalsha. It just hadn't been convenient. And there hadn't been anyone he was interested in enough to want to date. Besides the last time he'd indulged in anything close to a relationship was with Shana years ago and it had ended badly. Still here he was, lying in bed with a beautiful naked woman. Shana. There was simply no way he could not touch her. Her body was responding and he was ready. As soon as she turned toward him and kissed him, he kissed her back, rolled over on top of her and entered her. Their passions rose and they climaxed quickly.

"I'd love to wake up every morning like this," Kal said, lying on his back with Shana's head on his chest, still caressing her.

"Me, too," Shana said.

"Well, we'll have to see what we can do about that." Kal rose from the bed and headed to the bathroom. "Okay, if I use your shower?"

"Sure," Shana said, getting out of bed. She grabbed her robe, feeling a little shy about walking around naked in front of him. "There are towels under the sink."

"Thanks." Kal smiled at her as he closed the bathroom door.

Shana made the bed and picked up all their clothes lying scattered on the floor. She put hers away and laid his neatly on the bed. The water was off already. Wow! She realized men must really take short showers. The door opened and Kal walked out with a towel wrapped around his waist. He had a broad, tanned chest and a firm stomach. He looked good! He walked up and kissed her.

"It's all yours," he said and turned her toward the bathroom, patting her butt.

"Okay, but be warned my showers take more than five minutes," Shana teased and shut the door.

Shana stepped into the shower and let the hot water flow over her flushed body. It felt good. Good, yet not as good as the sex. She just plain felt fabulous, still she could not let herself get used to this. Not before they had a talk. She simply had to do it and this was as good of time as any. They were both in great moods and had experienced a fabulous night of sex or was it lovemaking? Did she love him? Had she gotten there yet? She wasn't sure. She knew she could certainly fall in love with him. She needed just a little more time. First, she needed to explain what she'd done. He'd said he loved her last night so hopefully he would be open to listening with an open mind and have a forgiving heart. Thirty minutes later, Shana emerged from the bathroom. Kal was in the living room watching the morning news. She quickly dressed in a pair of jeans and a tank top and went out to sit on the couch with him.

Kal kissed her. "You look great."

"Thanks," Shana said. "Kal," Shana started. She watched him as he looked at her expectantly.

"Yes?" he prodded.

"We have to talk. Things are moving quickly," she managed. This was so difficult.

Taking Chances

"You're right," he answered holding her hand in his. His phone was vibrating in his pocket. "First, I have to check this. I'm on call this morning." He pulled the phone out of his pocket and listened to his message. "I'm sorry, I have to go to the hospital. We'll have to finish this conversation later. I'll call you when I'm done." He stood up and pulled her against him, kissed her and left.

Shana sat back down on the couch. "Damn!" She'd wanted to get that conversation over with badly. Oh well, she'd tried and now she'd have to wait and hope she could get up enough courage to try again.

* * * *

What the Hell was he doing? What was he thinking? He definitely wasn't thinking at all, that was the problem. He could've called the hospital and taken care of the patient over the phone. But no, he was CHICKEN! He was afraid to hear her confession, because then he would have to make his own confession. Even though he felt guilty as Hell about not telling her, he was terrified of the conversation's outcome. Could they get past their past and still move on? She was right, they needed to talk. She'd tried to and he'd went running out the door. But maybe she really wasn't going to tell him about the abortion, maybe she just wanted to talk to him about how serious he was about the relationship. Sure, that's what it was. Women always got serious after you slept with them. Hell, he was serious, so what was the problem? He was damn serious, hadn't he told her he loved her last night? He did love her. She was the mother of his child. He would simply wait for her to bring it up again.

Kal pulled up at Sadie's to pick up Kalsha and walked up the driveway into the house.

"Daddy!" Kalsha yelled running to the door to hug him.

"Hi, Baby!" Kal said picking her up and planting kisses over her cheeks.

"Daddy home," Kalsha giggled, kissing his cheek back.

Sadie stood watching the happy reunion. "So you decided to show up after all."

"Sorry, Sadie."

"So tell me what happened," she said smiling at Kal. "It better be good!"

"It got late and I decided to spend the night with Shana."

"Well, then, you're off the hook for not calling."

"Sadie, you said not to worry if I didn't pick Kalsha up last night—didn't you?"

"Yes, I did. Just wanted to make sure where you were," Sadie said. "So how was it?"

"Sadie!" Kal stated. "You aren't serious are you?"

"Of course. I want every little detail!"

"A man never tells."

"Whatever! So at least tell me if this is getting serious yet," Sadie prompted, sitting down on the couch.

"I think so," Kal said thoughtfully. "I think I'm in love with her."

"Good." Sadie picked Kalsha up and gave her a kiss on the cheek. "We're going to get you a Mommy yet, Baby."

"Huge obstacle though. Shana and I need to have a talk. No, not a talk. It'll be more like confession time."

"No doubt that's going to be tough. But if she loves you, too—she does, doesn't she?" Sadie asked, stopping abruptly and watching Kal's face for an answer.

"I'm not sure. She hasn't said anything yet."

"Have you told her?"

"Sort of," he answered.

"How do you sort of tell her?"

"I told her, but she was sleeping."

"Oh … are you sure?"

"What? That I told her?"

"No. That she was sleeping?" Sadie asked to make him consider the possibility she might not have been.

"Not positive."

"Regardless, you need to tell her when she's awake."

Kal knew she was right and he knew Sadie knew she was right. Of course, she was a woman and all men knew that women were always right anyway. "She said we needed to talk and I got nervous. Luckily the hospital called so I said I had to go and left."

"Kal," Sadie said soothingly.

Taking Chances

"I got scared. Having a confessional conversation is real scary. Period."

"It has to be done."

"I'm not even sure that was what she wanted to talk about."

"What do you mean?"

"You know how women are."

"How are women?" Sadie asked, totally confused by the conversation now.

"Once you sleep with them, they get notions about marriage."

"I see. You think she wants to get married already. Probably not. Women like to be sure about it first."

"Really?"

"Maybe she just wanted to know if you wanted to date exclusively, to see what your intentions are," Sadie offered.

"I am only dating her."

"She doesn't know that unless you tell her."

"I think I want to marry her. She is so beautiful and loving. But then sometimes when I think about what she did I get so angry, I don't want to be with her."

"Forgiveness, Kal. You have to forgive her before you two have this confession talk."

"I know. I do forgive her every time I look at Kalsha. Then I'm thankful she gave birth to our beautiful daughter."

"Keep thinking about Kalsha and forgiveness and the dreaded talk will go fine," Sadie offered.

"It's still her call. I'm going to wait for her to bring it up."

"She did. Remember?"

"Okay. I'm going to wait for her to bring it up again, then."

"And you are not going to run out the door again. Right?" she asked.

"Yes, I promise," Kal said.

Sadie got Kalsha's bag ready. Kalsha was such a beautiful child. Whether her parents knew it or not, she was conceived in love. They just didn't know it at the time. Kal was walking to the Vet carrying the car seat in one hand and holding Kalsha's hand with the other, when she remembered to ask him about Thanksgiving. "Kal, what are your plans for Thanksgiving?" she asked walking toward him.

Kal strapped the car seat into the seat and then put Kalsha into the seat. He turned to Sadie, "No plans yet. Are you cooking dinner?"

"Yes. Maybe you want to invite Shana."

"Can't unless we have the confession talk first."

"Oh, right, because she doesn't know about Kalsha."

"Yes, and I don't think it will happen that quickly, still you never know." Kal got in, and he and Kalsha headed home.

Sadie walked back to the house. She was going to need to do some praying. There were three lost and lonely people who badly needed some angels holding their hands while they tried to mesh their lives together. They needed to open their hearts and be forgiving to each other. At least two of them needed to. The third one was patiently waiting for the other two to come to their senses. "Please, Lord, help them become a family," Sadie prayed softly.

*** * * ***

Kal drove home thinking about his conversation with Sadie. She was right. He knew it. He needed to pray to God and ask for the strength to get through that dreaded conversation. No, confession. He needed a forgiving heart. He needed to stay focused on that part especially. God already forgave her and so he also needed to. If God could forgive her, there was absolutely no reason for him not to. Kal prayed softly, "God, please forgive me for what part I played in this mess and help me to forgive Shana. And please give me the strength and wisdom to do whatever I need to do to correct the situation now."

Kal called Shana after he drove home and put Kalsha to bed. They talked on the phone. He couldn't take her out or go over to her place now because he had Kalsha. Sadie and Mac had a party to attend, so he was staying home. He didn't mind, yet he couldn't tell her the reason. That made it difficult. So they talked on the phone. The Vikings were playing on Sunday though, and he was taking her to the End Zone bar again to watch the game. He missed her. He wanted to be with her. He missed touching her. Finally, their conversation ended and Kal was lying in bed alone, completely aroused. He forced himself to stop thinking about Shana's naked body. It was tough but he finally

Taking Chances

succeeded and drifted off to sleep.

* * * *

Shana was looking forward to the Vikings game and especially to seeing Kal. She thought it was odd he hadn't come over on Saturday night. He said he just got home from the hospital when he called her last night. Oh, well, she didn't want to be a needy girlfriend. She would see him any minute, since he was picking her up to go watch the game. She was dressed in her Vikings shirt and cap, ready to go, when he knocked at her door.

"Come in," she yelled out from the bedroom.

Kal walked in and towards the bedroom where her voice came from. He took her in his arms and kissed her thoroughly. "I missed you," he said against her ear.

"I missed you, too," Shana said.

Kal was hard-pressed to let her go and walk out of the bedroom. The bed looked inviting and reminded him of the crazy lovemaking, just the other night. He took her hand. "We better get going so we don't miss the kick off."

Shana picked up her purse and keys. "I'm ready," she said, opening the door and locking it behind them as they left.

The bar was even more packed then the last time they were there, probably because it was a Sunday game. They squeezed their way to the back table where Kal's friends were waiting.

"About time you guys got here, they're about to start the kick off," Tom said, pulling out chairs for them.

Shana chatted with Susie and Bonnie, feeling she knew them at least a little bit this time. They were both so open and friendly. Conversation was tough, though, with all the cheering and noise in the bar. The Vikings scored and Shana joined the cheering, jumping up out of her chair with the others.

Kal caught her around the waist pulling her to him. He gave her a quick kiss and whispered in her ear, "Can't wait until later."

Shana wasn't sure what he meant, though she hoped it meant he would be spending the night with her again. She smiled and said, "Me, too."

It was an exciting game, with a tied score until the last minute when the Vikings scored a touchdown to win the game.

They left as soon as the game was over, saying their good-byes to Kal's friends. Shana watched Kal, throughout the game. He was definitely a good-looking man. She watched women check him out as they walked through the bar. Kal, however, hadn't acknowledged their bold appraisals at all. Instead, he placed his hand on her side, guiding her to the door, so everyone knew she was with him. She felt proud to be with him. He was a good man. She got in the car while Kal held the door open for her. Did she dare call him her boyfriend?

After arriving at her parking lot, he walked with her to her apartment. This felt awkward. Did she invite him in or did she assume he would come in? Heck, she didn't know, so she said, "It's early, so do you want to come in for a while?"

"Thought you'd never ask!" Kal grinned, picked her up and twirled her around.

Shana buried her head in his shoulder and protested, "Hey, I'm getting dizzy."

"Wouldn't want that," Kal said, stopping and kissing her instead, while she unlocked the door so they could go inside her apartment.

Shana's body warmed to his caresses and soon there was a trail of clothes leading to the bedroom. Adrenaline was high from the excitement of the game and the sex was intense. Later, they both lay sated on the bed.

"Unbelievably intense," Kal said.

"Totally," she agreed.

"Do you want to go steady?" Kal said looking at her with a serious stare.

"Do people still do that?" Shana asked, unsure if he was serious or only kidding around.

"Not sure," he said with a smirk on his face.

"You are kidding, right?"

"Sort of. I do want us to date exclusively. Is that okay with you?"

"That would make me unbelievably happy!" Shana stated.

"Well, then, that's settled," Kal said and pulled her to him. He kissed her to seal the deal.

Taking Chances

"Sealed with a kiss," Shana whispered up against his ear.
"Isn't that a song?" Kal asked.
"A classic. I love that song," Shana answered.

Chapter Thirteen

Kal didn't spend the night. He hated to leave, but he'd promised Sadie to pick up Kalsha. He knew Shana wanted him to stay even though she didn't say anything. He told her he didn't think he should stay since they both had to be at work in the morning. It was one of the hardest things he'd had to do—leave her bed to go home.

At the hospital the next morning, all he could think of was Shana. He definitely had it bad. He was in love. No ifs, ands, or buts about it. He was hooked. Now what was he going to do about it? Maybe he could simply take her to Las Vegas and get married. Then, later, they could have the confession talk. Unfortunately, they had to have the talk before he could introduce her to Kalsha, so that was probably a bad plan.

He called Shana every night and they went to dinner on Wednesday night. Then back to her place to make love to his woman. Yes, now it was making love not just having sex.

Saturday afternoon he picked Shana up to go to an Art Fair in Old Scottsdale. They parked and proceeded to walk up and down the aisles of Art and Craft booths.

"This is so much fun, Kal. Thanks for taking me."

"My pleasure," Kal said.

They walked down more aisles and stopped to look at the artist's displays. Shana particularly liked the jewelry displays.

"This is a very unique piece of turquoise," Shana said as she stopped to look in a glass case. It was a slide shaped like a heart on a silver chain.

"Do you like it?" Kal asked, looking it over and checking the price.

Taking Chances

"Yes, it's very different."

"Try it on," Kal urged.

Shana put the chain on and looked at it in the mirror. She liked what she saw.

"If you want it, I'll buy it for you," Kal offered.

"Are you sure?" she asked taking it off and setting it on the counter.

"We'll take it," Kal said. The clerk wrapped up the slide with the chain and charged it to Kal's credit card. He signed for it and handed Shana the bag.

"I don't know what to say. Thank you." She leaned over and kissed him on the cheek.

"You're welcome," Kal said and they continued walking through the art fair, holding hands.

They stopped at the food concession area to eat, opting for pizza and salad. For dessert, gelato. The sun was setting so they took the leisurely way home, driving with the top down.

Shana barely contained her excitement. It was Saturday night and Kal would be spending the night. The day had been great. She loved art fairs and this was her first one in Phoenix. The gift was unexpected though greatly appreciated, mainly because it was a necklace she could wear and be reminded of Kal. The warm wind was blowing and gently caressed her face. Soon Kal would be caressing her body and heat flared through her body.

"What do you want to do tonight?" Kal asked after they arrived at her apartment.

"Watch TV?"

"Anything else?" Kal drew closer, wound one arm around her waist and pulled him to her, then kissed her soundly.

"Go to bed?" she asked.

"Good answer. Which order?"

"We could go to bed and see if anything comes up—"

Kal's eyebrows shot up and Shana laughed and ran for the bedroom with Kal close behind.

"You better run, because that something has come up already." Kal was quickly undressing while he watched Shana strip off her clothes.

He stopped to stare at her naked body. "Damn! You're so beautiful, Shana."

She stopped and looked at him admiring her with his eyes. "You look pretty good naked yourself."

"Come here," Kal said as he kneeled on the bed.

She came to him and he traced his finger along her face, cupping her chin to bring her lips to his for a soul-searching kiss. He ran his fingers along her neck and down her sides.

He reached for her breasts cupping them and sucking each one gently. She reached for him and stroked him with a slow caressing motion. Their bodies moved together in harmonious unison. He laid her down on the bed, and held himself over her as he pressed against her entrance. He teased, entering only a little and withdrawing, entering a little more and withdrawing. Shana's body writhed below him, arching towards his rock hard shaft seeking her heat. He held back, kissed her lips and sent his tongue dancing inside her mouth, then sucking her lower lip. Her body was arching wildly toward him. He couldn't hold back any longer. He entered her body, slowly, enjoying every minute of the entrance, and then increasing the momentum, racing to the finish. Taking them both to explosive climaxes simultaneously. Kal rolled over and pulled Shana to face him.

"I love you, Shana," Kal said looking into her beautiful eyes.

"I love you, too," Shana replied, and her eyes lit up as she spoke the words out loud for the first time in her life.

They fell asleep in each other's arms, both feeling completely loved and at peace with the world. At least for now.

* * * *

Morning arrived with Shana still wrapped in Kal's arms. She woke up with a smile. "Good morning," she said.

"Good morning. What are your plans for today?"

"I have no plans."

"You know, Thanksgiving is this Thursday. What will you be doing?"

"I actually hadn't thought about it."

"I'm on call during the day," Kal said.

Taking Chances

"Oh," she said, slightly disappointed.
"Are you up for cooking dinner?"
"I can. Will you be here for dinner?"
"If you make it after five, I can."
"It's a date," Shana said happily.

* * * *

Shana cooked all day making the traditional Thanksgiving meal of turkey, dressing, green bean casserole, mashed potatoes, stuffing, gravy, cranberries, rolls, and pumpkin pie. Although she cheated on the pie and bought one already made from Coco's. Their pies were always delicious, and probably much better than one she could make. The little local bakery, The Bake Shop, had great fresh breads so she ordered a package of dinner rolls from them.

She'd never cooked a Thanksgiving dinner all by herself, so this was a first. The cooking channel shows ran specials on how to cook a great Thanksgiving meal so she taped them and took notes as she watched. Supposedly, these were all tricks of the trade, such as putting slices of butter under the skin of the turkey breast, adding cinnamon to the cranberry sauce and making the mashed potatoes the night before with sour cream and cream cheese.

Tara had a great recipe for a green bean casserole she always bragged about, so Shana emailed her to get it.

Everything went as planned and she was pleased with her cooking ability. Heck, it was totally a meat and potatoes meal, which was definitely Minnesotan so she was confident she could cook it. Hours later, it was all under control and she had the table set and the food ready when Kal arrived. Gravy was always tricky, so she was glad she'd opted to use the packages. She even got daring and mixed it in with the gravy bag that came with the turkey, along with mixing in the drippings from the turkey. The gravy actually tasted pretty good, she thought after she sampled it.

"Smells great," Kal said, getting a whiff of the turkey.

"Help me a minute. Everything's ready, we just need to put it all on the table."

Kal helped carry the serving dishes filled with the hot food, then they sat down and ate their mouthwatering Thanksgiving dinner.

"Everything tastes great. I have always loved the green bean casserole. I think it is a Minnesotan thing," Kal complimented Shana.

"I got the recipe from my friend Tara, from Minnesota," Shana stated.

"It tasted exactly like the one my grandmother used to make," Kal said. He knew at that moment he wanted to marry Shana and make the three of them a family. Kal, Shana, and Kalsha.

After the meal was over, Kal helped Shana clear the table and load the dishwasher. Shana filled storage containers with the leftovers before they retired to the couch in front of the TV to have the pumpkin pie for dessert. Kal picked up the remote and turned the television on to watch the news but kept the volume down low.

"Shana, I like being with you. I love making love to you. And I want to spend the rest of my life with you."

Shana was stunned. "Are you asking me to marry you?"

"I guess it's kind of a pre-proposal."

"So you know the answer before you do the actual proposal. I get it."

"And your answer would be?"

"I can't think of anything I'd rather do than spend my life with you, Kal."

Kal was ecstatic. They still had to have the confession talk, however he was feeling confident everything was going to work out just fine. He needed to buy an engagement ring and come up with a great proposal plan. Life was looking exceptionally well today. Kal took her hand and led her to the bedroom where they spent the night making love.

In the morning, Kal left to make his rounds at the hospital with a turkey sandwich Shana made for him. After rounds, he drove home to see Kalsha where Sadie would be dropping her off shortly after he arrived.

"So how was your Thanksgiving?" Sadie asked.

"One I'll never forget."

"That good, huh?" Sadie asked.

Taking Chances

"I want to marry her."

"Wow! Must've been some Thanksgiving dinner."

"Her cooking was pretty good, too," Kal added.

"I have to go. Mac is waiting in the car. Still have some more Black Friday sales to hit. We'll talk later," Sadie said.

"Thanks, Sadie."

"No problem. You know we love taking care of Kalsha," Sadie said and rushed out the door.

Kal picked Kalsha up and smothered her with kisses. He'd missed his baby girl.

* * * *

Saturday night Kal picked Shana up. There were four new releases and they picked the new Mission Impossible movie. Afterwards they grabbed a late dinner at the Cheesecake Factory. Cheesecake always sounded good, especially with fresh strawberries generously draping the original cheesecake and plate along with a dab of whipped cream.

The pool in Shana's apartment complex was empty and inviting as they drove by on their way to her apartment.

"Too bad you don't have a swimsuit or we could take a quick dip," Shana said.

"Oh, but I do."

"Really?"

"Just happen to have my gym bag and I always have one in it."

"Want to check it out?"

"Most definitely."

A few minutes later, they were walking to the pool with towels in hand. It was a beautiful, clear, slightly chilly night, and the sky was filled with stars, but the pool was heated and then of course there was the hot tub.

Kal dove in. Shana took the steps, slowly entering the pool while he intently watched her every move. He swam up to her, pulling her to him for a deep kiss. Then he tugged on the back string of her bikini while he watched her breasts release into his eagerly waiting hands.

Before she knew, her bikini and his swim trunks were in a pile on the side of the pool and Kal was thrusting against her pelvis and entering her primed body that matched his movements thrust for thrust. His mouth devoured hers and they climaxed with an intensity overwhelming them both.

"Wow!" she gasped in his ear.

"Wow is right," Kal whispered.

"Never did it in a pool before," Shana said.

"Me either, but I think we'll have to make a habit of it," Kal said.

"I agree."

They put their suits back on and walked back to her apartment. Shana attempted to put some clothes on after they were in her apartment, however Kal caught her naked body in his arms and carried her to the bed.

"You didn't think we were done, did you?" he asked.

"I guess we're not," Shana said and rolled over on top of Kal.

* * * *

Shana was on top of the world when she walked into the hospital on Monday morning. She'd been semi-proposed to. Was that even a real word? Kal would be her husband and they would spend their lives together. She couldn't tell anyone until he actually proposed. She wasn't sure when it would take place, however she hoped it was soon. Her mood dropped slightly when she recalled the talk they still needed to have. Maybe it could wait until later.

Shana walked into the main reception lobby of the hospital.

"Good morning, Shana. How was your Thanksgiving?" the receptionist asked.

"It was one of the best Thanksgivings I've ever had."

"Did you cook or go out for dinner?"

"I cooked," Shana said, not sure if she should say Kal was there or not.

"I hope you didn't spend it alone."

"I cooked dinner for Dr. Paxton." Shana decided it should be all right since they would be getting engaged soon and everyone at the hospital would know then.

"I know he had to work on Thanksgiving, so I'm glad he got to have a home cooked meal. Did he bring his daughter?"

Taking Chances

"No," Shana said, after a short hesitation. Patients approached the desk and Shana walked away, stunned. She walked slowly back to her office, practically collapsing in her chair. Kal had a child? Why hadn't he told her? Hadn't he just proposed to her? Asked her to spend her life with him? She had a right to know he had a child, didn't she? Of course she did. Didn't he have faith in her? Didn't he think she would accept his child? Why hadn't he told her? They had to talk, but right now, she had work to do, so she had to get a grip and focus on her job. She would discuss this with Kal after work.

Shana regrouped and focused on her schedule for the day. She emailed Kal stating she needed to talk to him, in person, after work. He sent her an email back saying to meet him in the parking lot when she was done. The day dragged but she made it through.

At five, she walked out of her office, scared to death. She tried to tell herself it would be okay. There was a good reason he hadn't told her. She walked out the door and straight to the parking lot to Kal's car. He was standing next to it watching her and smiling. He walked towards her and took her in his arms for a hug.

"I missed you," he said. Then he must have noticed her serious look. "Are you okay?"

She had to get to the point; she couldn't take the suspense any longer. "Kal, do you have a daughter?" she asked, so nervous, she was shaking.

Kal's mind was racing. Someone at the hospital must have told her something. Oh, well, he would've had to tell her eventually anyway. He just hoped she was going to accept it well. "Yes."

Kal was praying she wouldn't freak out. He was pretty sure she only knew he had a daughter and didn't know Kalsha was *her* daughter, too. Because only he, Sadie and Mac knew who Kalsha's mother was.

"Why didn't you tell me?"

"I wanted you to fall in love with me first. I didn't want to scare you away because I had a child. I'm sorry."

"Is that why you did a pre-proposal?"

That was good, he should've thought of that. "Yes."

"How old is she?"

"Two."

"What's her name?"

"Kalsha," Kal answered hoping she wouldn't realize it was a combination of his name and hers.

"Can I meet her?"

"Of course. I have to pick her up at my sister, Sadie's house. I'll give you directions to my house and you can meet me there."

"Okay." That was all she could manage to say at the moment. Kal wrote down the directions and handed them to her.

"I'll be there in an hour. It takes an hour with the traffic. See you there," Kal said and got into his car.

Shana walked to her car and got in, but was still shaking. Why, she wasn't sure. Deep breaths, that's what she needed. She took deep breaths and finally relaxed a little and managed to stop shaking. This was all about a child—a small child. Everything would be fine. She read the directions and started driving.

She wasn't sure why she was surprised when she turned into the Silverton executive neighborhood. The house was large and breathtakingly beautiful. It was a sprawling two story in a brown stone exterior with bronze double entrance doors. Massive gardens and palm trees lined the entrance along with a water fountain and stone benches. Kal was a doctor, after all, what had she expected? She sat in her car waiting for Kal to arrive, preparing herself to meet Kal's child.

Twenty minutes later, Kal's car pulled up in the driveway and one of the four garage doors opened. Shana got out of her car and walked up Kal's long driveway to face her immense fear, which consisted of meeting one very special small child. Kal's daughter.

Shana watched as Kal pulled a small beautiful child from her car seat and set her on the driveway facing Shana.

"Shana, this is Kalsha," Kal said.

Shana walked towards them, and Kalsha walked over to meet her. She stopped and bent down to greet Kalsha. "Hello," Shana said and held out her hands. Kalsha walked right into her arms, hugged her, and planted a big kiss on Shana's cheek.

Kal chuckled. "She's very friendly."

"I see that." Shana hugged the child back before releasing her.

Taking Chances

"Would you like to see my house? Please come in," Kal invited. He picked up Kalsha and opened the front door to the house.

Shana followed them inside. She stood in a long foyer reaching to the back of the house where a wall of windows looked down on the valley below and the Superstition Mountains painted a beautiful backdrop. The back room was a massive open room for the kitchen, eating area and family room which led to a stone patio, the size of her entire apartment, complete with an outdoor kitchen, pool and hot tub, landscaped perfectly with three water fountains surrounded by palm trees and desert greenery.

"This is beautiful, Kal." She watched the child who had blonde hair, a round face with a beautiful smile and amber brown eyes. In fact, they were the same color as Shana's. She was mesmerized, watching the happy child sitting on the floor playing with toys, holding a baby doll. She took a seat on a couch.

She knew Kal was watching her as she watched Kalsha. He said nothing. Her mind was reeling. Did she still want to spend her life with Kal? Could she be a mother to this child? What kind of mother would she be? Her abortion scared her, so what did that say about her, about the kind of woman she was? The kind of mother she would make? Until she knew those answers, she couldn't be anyone's mother. Besides, she and Kal hadn't even discussed having children.

Did she even want to be a mother? She actually hadn't given it any thought, in fact, she probably had deliberately not thought about it. She loved Kal, but was she ready for this? Would she have gone out with him if she'd known? The answer was yes. She was so strongly attracted to him and she felt an unexplainable bond with Kal. She couldn't explain what it was—it was simply there. It had felt comfortable to hold Kalsha, too. Why? Maybe because of the bond with Kal.

"Shana?" Kal said breaking her trance-like state. He'd been watching her sitting on the couch perfectly still, staring at Kalsha. "Are you okay?"

Shana looked at him. "This is all quite a shock." She stood up and walked towards Kalsha. Kalsha looked up at her. For a moment, she was reminded of one of her own baby pictures. Kalsha reminded her of herself. Their colorings were the same—hair, eyes and skin. "She's a beautiful child." She moved to Kal's side. He put his arms around her and hugged her tightly, pressing her to him.

"I love you, Shana," he said leaning back a little to look into her face. He kissed her gently. "I'm sorry I didn't tell you. I wanted to, however I wanted you to fall in love with me first."

"I love you, Kal," Shana said, and hugged him tightly placing her head on his shoulder. "We never talked about having children."

"I know. Do you want children, Shana?"

"Yes. I do but I'm not so sure I am ready yet."

"I'm not so sure anyone ever truly is. It certainly changes your life. Nonetheless Kalsha is a very loving and happy child."

"I can see that." Shana turned and looked at Kalsha. Unfortunately watching Kalsha made her think about her baby that never was born. Correction, her, and Kal's baby. She wondered what their child would have looked like. Actually, it could've looked like Kalsha, because Kalsha resembled her own baby pictures. Tears were flooding her eyes. She wiped them away quickly. She walked towards the front door and Kal followed her. "I have to go."

"Shana, are you all right, maybe we should talk this out?" He came up behind her and gently massaged her tense shoulders.

"Yes, we should, but not now. I need some time alone to sort out my feelings."

"Okay, if you think that's best," Kal said.

"We'll talk later." Shana swiped at the tears rolling down her cheeks. She opened the door. "I have one question, though. Where is Kalsha's mother?"

Kal was afraid to let her go. He was even more afraid to answer her question, so he chose his words carefully. He didn't want to lie to her anymore, however this was not the time for confessions. "Unfortunately, she wasn't ready to be a mother when Kalsha was born."

Shana gasped, "I have to go," and practically ran down the driveway to her car.

Kal watched helplessly as she left, hoping everything would work out in the end. At least she seemed to accept his answer about Kalsha's

Taking Chances

mother. He was so torn. He wanted to go after her yet he knew she needed some time alone.

He walked back inside and closed the door. Kalsha was walking down the hall looking for him.

"Daddy?" Kalsha said.

"Daddy's here, Kalsha baby." Kal picked her up and showered her with kisses. Kisses for her and Shana. The phone ringing interrupted him.

"Hello."

"Kal, are you alright? How'd she take it?" Sadie asked.

"She left."

"What happened?"

"I introduced her to Kalsha."

"And she left right away?"

"No. She held Kalsha. She seemed dazed and I could tell her thoughts were reeling. She simply sat on the couch staring at Kalsha and not saying anything."

"And then?"

"I told her I loved her."

"That's a good start."

"She said she loved me, too, but wasn't sure she was ready to be a mother."

"I'm sure this was a huge shock for her."

"Said she needed time. Do you think I've lost her again?"

"I hope not. If she told you she loved you that's a good sign."

"Maybe I shouldn't have let her go, Sadie?"

"This is a difficult situation. Give her some time."

"Sadie, she asked who Kalsha's mother was."

"And?"

"I told her she wasn't ready to be a mother at the time. I couldn't lie to her."

"That was a good answer. I'm assuming you didn't feel it was the right time to confess the truth?"

"Hell, this wasn't the way I wanted this to go down. I wanted to talk to her about everything first."

"Well yes, that would've probably been better, although it's too late now."

"Right."

"Remember, she has a confession to make, too. Give her time to digest this part of the relationship. Then you two need to have a serious talk, and the truth from both of you must be revealed."

"She liked my house, Sadie."

"Hey, that's something, then again who wouldn't?" Sadie teased. "Call me if you need me to watch Kalsha. No matter what time of day or night it is."

"Thanks, Sadie." Kal hung up the phone and turned to Kalsha.

"So that was your mommy, Shana, what do you think of her?"

"Mommy?" Kalsha asked.

"Yes, Mommy. Wasn't she pretty?"

"Pretty Mommy," Kalsha repeated.

"I love you, Baby," Kal said, hugging Kalsha.

He looked at the phone, desperately wanting to pick it up and call Shana. But she'd just left and she needed time. Surely, thirty minutes didn't count as long enough. Nonetheless how long was long enough- an hour, hours, a day, days? How long did he wait before he called her? Was there a rulebook on this? How were men supposed to know what to do if there weren't any rules to go by? He missed her already. It was Monday, so maybe by Wednesday he could call her? He could email her though, right. That was it; he'd email her something short, tomorrow at work.

* * * *

Shana drove home. She wasn't sure exactly how she got there because her mind was focused on Kal and his daughter. She walked into her apartment, dropped the keys on the coffee table along with her purse and sank down on the couch. What had just happened? She wasn't sure. She'd been so happy when she'd gone to work at the hospital this morning. Then shortly after arriving at work, her world came tumbling down, all because of a small child. Shana didn't have anything against the child. In fact, Kalsha was an adorable child. Beautiful and loving. So why was she so upset? There were many single parents around today, and she was sure the odds were high the person you dated would have children. Well, maybe not high, yet definitely a possibility. Was it really about the child, or her? So what if Kal had had a child with someone else? She and Kal could have their own children, too. It wasn't that at all. Every time she looked at Kalsha, she was reminded of what she'd done. She had to tell him. Only she wasn't so sure she could tell him in person now. She was scared, but it had to be done. She was drained mentally and she didn't want to think about it anymore right now.

She reached for the TV remote control, turned it on, flipping through channel after channel until one interested her. A mindless show, she could tune out was what she needed. Her mind was still focused on how she was going to tell Kal what she'd done. She really didn't think she could do it face to face, so she'd either have to call him, write a letter or send him an email. A letter sounded good. Once that was decided, Shana fell asleep on the couch for the night.

Sometime during the night, she must've moved to the bedroom, because the alarm clock was buzzing next to her head. She reached over and turned it off. It was a new day and maybe the answers to her predicament would come to her somehow.

Chapter Fourteen

Kal arrived at work the next morning, and scanned the parking lot for a glimpse of Shana. He saw her car, so he knew she must've already arrived. He walked in and scanned the hallways in hope of seeing her, but no such luck. She was probably already in her office. The first thing he did after sitting down at his desk was check his emails. He knew he was hoping there would be one from her, but no luck—again. He so badly wanted to send her an email right now, however he needed to show some restraint and at least wait until the end of the day. He glanced at the phone wanting to call her. He had a full schedule, so it was best to only concentrate on work and hopefully it would take his mind off Shana.

The day passed and he didn't see her and she didn't email him. He knew she wouldn't be leaving for a half hour, so he sat down to email her.

Shana,
I know I need to give you time, so I'm going to send you this email. I miss you. I am sorry for not telling you about Kalsha. When you are ready to talk, call me anytime. Anytime. It's your call. I'll wait to hear from you.
Kal

He pressed the send button. The computer confirmed it was sent. Minutes later an email from Shana came through.

Taking Chances

Kal,
I miss you. I'll call you when I'm ready to talk. Please be patient with me.
Shana

Kal leaned back in his chair and sighed. Well, at least she'd answered his email. That was good, he suspected. Patience. He needed lots of it. The radio played in the background. An advertisement for diamond rings caught his attention. Diamond rings for engagements. He got out of his chair, closed up his office and walked out of the building to his car. He was now a man on a mission. He was going to buy Shana an engagement ring. Just in case this whole thing worked out, he wanted to be prepared. He wanted to propose to her properly and make it special so she would always remember it.

* * * *

Shana received Kal's email late in the day. She'd wanted to talk to him still she wasn't ready for the conversation that needed to come first. She'd asked for time and now it was her call. She stood staring out her office window. Kal would be leaving about now, so she would wait a little bit before she left. Picking up a pen and paper, she sat down in her chair. This was as good a time as any to write down her confession. Actually writing it down would be the best way. Where to start?—at the beginning of course.

Dear Kal,
This is the second hardest thing I have ever had to do. If after you read this, you still want me, I am yours. However, I must tell you of the unforgiveable thing I have done. Unfortunately first I need to tell you what led up to all this.
You remember the night we met? I had just lost my job and was feeling sorry for myself. My mother, who was my best friend, had recently died and the day we met, I was laid off from my job. I know

that's no excuse, but I was at the bar trying to get drunk, which isn't my style at all, and then you sat down next to me. You know what happened after that and how you came home with me.

What you don't know is that I got pregnant that night. I didn't realize it right away because I was suffering from depression. Thanks to the pregnancy tests now available at the pharmacy stores, I found out for sure. I was forced to make an appointment at a free clinic because I had no insurance and ended up being exposed to German measles. I was so scared, Kal, for me and the baby. The nurse at the free clinic painted an ugly picture of what the chances of a healthy baby could be. I didn't know what to do. I didn't have anyone to talk to. I waited and agonized over my decision. You have to believe me.

But what was I to do? I couldn't support myself much less a child with major medical problems. Especially without a job or insurance. I did the unthinkable. However, at the last minute, I tried, I really did try to change my mind unfortunately it was too late. I was already sedated and when I woke up it was over. The abortion was done. I don't know if I can ever forgive myself. I went through counseling sessions with Tara at New Beginnings Clinic during this time and hope to come to terms with my decision someday.

I don't expect you to forgive me. Only understand that if I could undo what I did, I would. I love you and I only hope after you read this, that you'll find it in your heart to forgive me or at least understand the circumstances surrounding that life changing day.

Love,
Shana

Shana sat back in the chair. She felt a sense of relief wash over her. There it was on paper. Once again, she read it over making sure everything was right. She thought about typing it into the computer but decided this was probably better being hand written. Then she signed it, folded it and put it in an envelope, licking it shut and putting his name on the front—Kal Paxton. She set it down on the work area counter, went to get her purse, and got her keys out. It was about six thirty when she drove home.

Taking Chances

After a restless sleepless night, she arrived at work, extremely tired the next morning. Meg was already there when she arrived. Shana was a bit late because she'd stopped at Starbuck's on the way to pick up a Mocha Frappuccino, hoping the caffeine in it would wake her up. She quickly looked at her calendar, realizing she'd almost forgot her nine thirty meeting, so she grabbed her files and flew out the door and down the hall.

It was the Christmas party committee meeting to finalize the party details. The party was being held mid-January so people didn't have to worry about conflicts with everything else going on in December. The meeting was relaxed because they still had plenty of time to finish up the arrangements. Thankfully, the meeting flowed smoothly because she was struggling to stay focused.

She was tired when she walked back into her office after the meeting. She didn't want to think about the letter, or when she'd give it or send it to Kal. The problem with the mail was you never knew when the other person would receive it and that was a problem, when technically you were dropping a bomb. Maybe handing it to him was the best approach. And then of course leave before he read it. She scanned her desk. Where was it? She'd left it there hadn't she? No, not on her desk, but the work area counter. She looked over in that direction quickly and realized she'd left it right in front of the inter office mail basket. It wasn't there and the basket was empty.

"Meg? Did you see an envelope for Kal?"

"Yes, it was lying in front of the inter office basket so I grabbed it when I took the rest of the inter office mail downstairs to the mail room while you were at your meeting. He'll have it this afternoon."

Shana didn't respond. Her heart was pounding wildly in her chest. She wanted to hand it to him personally, not have it delivered. Her head was throbbing now, too. She didn't think she could face him after all. Meg's phone rang so at least she didn't have to respond to Meg. There were only a few more things she needed to take care of before she could leave. She needed to send Kal an email before she left.

Rose Marie Meuwissen

Kal,
There are some things you need to know about me before we can even think about having a life together. I felt it was best done by writing it down in a letter. You should receive it this afternoon. Please have an open mind and heart when you read it.
I love you.
Shana

Shana took a deep breath and sighed as she slowly pressed the send button. Her fate was now in God's hands, so why was she scared to death and wanting to do nothing except run as far away as possible from Kal, the hospital and Arizona? She couldn't wait around to hear Kal tell her how he never wanted to see her again. There was simply no way in her mind he was going to be understanding and forgive her for what she'd done. He would no longer want to marry her. Her thoughts were going crazy. At three, she walked out of the hospital early and drove home.

She tried to make sense of the scenarios going through her head as she drove. When she got home, she went directly to the computer. This was just not something she was ready to face today. She went online and booked a flight to Minneapolis for the next morning. Fortunately, she got a really low price for an air ticket, hotel and car. Thank heavens because otherwise she wouldn't have been able to afford it. She sent Tara an email to let her know she was coming and headed into the bedroom to pack a bag. Hopefully, Kal would be so upset he wouldn't call her tonight.

Bags packed, she slid into the bed, exhausted. She would call work in the morning before she left for the airport. Her heart was breaking into a million pieces. Even though she didn't want to talk to Kal, the sheer reality he hadn't even bothered to call, hurt. Really hurt! She closed her eyes and cleared her mind so she could finally fall asleep.

* * * *

Kal walked into the jewelry store. He didn't actually look at the settings because he wanted Shana with him to pick the wedding ring.

Taking Chances

The sales person brought unset diamonds out for him to look at and explained all about the 4-C's of diamonds. Color, clarity, cut and carat size. It was truly a learning experience. Who would've thought you needed to know all about diamonds to pick out a ring? After listening to the sales person's info on diamonds and looking at many different sizes and shapes, he picked a beautiful sparkling round two carat, high quality stone and had it set in a gold solitaire.

Kal walked out of the jewelry store carrying the key to his future. This would seal the deal for his and Kalsha's life together with Shana. A grin spread across his face. He got into his car one happy man and extremely confident this would work out.

When he arrived at his sister's house, Sadie met Kal at the door. "Anything new happen?"

"I emailed her and she emailed me back."

"Good, I think."

"She needs more time but will call when she's ready to talk."

"Good. And then you're going to tell her everything, right?"

"Yes, we have to talk about it."

"You know there is a chance she may leave you after your confession, don't you?"

"Yes, but I hope not. I plan to seal the deal first," Kal said, smiling.

"How are you going to do that?"

"With this." Kal pulled out the ring box from his pocket and handed it to Sadie.

She opened it. "Kal! It's beautiful."

"Do you think it will seal the deal?"

"This will certainly make her think twice about leaving. It will show you are willing to make a lifetime commitment to her." Sadie put the ring back in the box and handed it to Kal. "Good job. I'm proud of you. This is a big step. Are you done working for the day?"

"No, I need to stop at the hospital to check on one of my patients. I'll be back as soon as I can."

"Daddy," Kalsha said running to him from the other room.

He reached down for Kalsha and picked her up. "Shana accepting this ring is the key to my future and Kalsha's."

* * * *

Later in the day, Kal stopped back at the hospital and walked into his office to find an envelope lying in the middle of his desk. He walked slowly toward it, sensing it was from Shana. Picking up the envelope, he took his time opening it slowly and sat down in his chair to read it. His eyes watered as he read her confession. Most of what she'd wrote he already knew however some he didn't. He hadn't realized how much she'd suffered and how much he'd contributed to her pain. She'd carried this pain and guilt inside her for over two years. He needed to talk to her and tell her his part in what had happened.

Kal set the letter down and leaned back in his chair, running his fingers through his hair. He glanced at the computer and saw he had an email. It was from Shana. He read it and felt her uncertainty, pain, and yet the hope in her words. He sent a return email asking if she was online. There was no response. He called her extension and got her voicemail. It was almost five so she could have left already. He was unsure of what to do next.

Maybe Sadie would have some insight as to what his next move should be. He drove up her driveway feeling hopeful.

Sadie opened her door and immediately knew something had happened. "Kal, are you okay?" she asked, concerned.

"Shana sent me her confession in a letter."

"Oh, Kal," she said hugging him.

"I have put her through pure Hell."

"What?"

"I had her sedated during the procedure so she wouldn't realize what I was doing."

"Okay, but you knew that so what is the problem now?"

"She changed her mind right before the sedation took effect. So if I hadn't ordered her to be sedated, she would've called it off and kept Kalsha."

"You already knew that, right?" Sadie questioned.

"My nurse heard it from the nurse who stayed with Shana that night. I just was never sure if it was really true. Now I know it was," Kal said.

"Have you talked to her?"

Taking Chances

"No. She didn't answer her email or phone, so I'm assuming she'd already left for the day."

"Maybe you should wait until tomorrow to talk to her?"

"Maybe. But I think I'll call her after Kalsha and I get home."

Sadie handed Kalsha and her bag to Kal. "Hang in there, Kal. I have a feeling this is all going to work out."

"Let's hope so," Kal said, walking to the car.

After putting Kalsha to bed, he sat on the couch rereading her letter. This time as he read Shana's heartfelt words, his eyes watered and he allowed himself to cry. He'd hurt her so much. He should've been there for her. Helped her. Their lives could've been so different. He was going to make this up to her. They were going to be a family and he was going to take care of her.

It was only nine thirty, so he called her number. She didn't answer instead he got her voicemail. He chose not to leave a message because he wanted to talk to her not a machine, so he hung up. He was going to assume she was already sleeping. Mainly because the other alternatives, he didn't like at all. She could possibly not be there, or the even worse possibility was she was choosing not to answer. He would call again in the morning.

* * * *

The alarm rang bright and early at four in the morning. Shana reluctantly got up to shower and get ready. She dressed and waited for the airport shuttle to pick her up. While she was waiting, she called her manager at the hospital to say she needed a few days off to go back to Minnesota to take care of some pressing unfinished business.

Two hours later she was boarding a plane headed to Denver and then would be catching a connecting flight to Minneapolis. She took her seat, a window seat, and noticed the empty middle seat. Maybe she would get lucky and it would be empty. She took her cell phone out of her purse and checked to see if there were any messages. None. Then she checked the missed call list and saw his number. He'd called but hadn't left a message. Her heart sank. Maybe she should call him after she landed in Minneapolis? She needed to talk to Tara, because Tara would know what she should do. She was so confused right now. She loved Kal, only would he ever forgive her? That was the question. She would have to face him eventually, but not today. Today she was going back home. She turned her phone off and put it back in her purse.

* * * *

Kal slept very little. He tossed and turned and his mind went over and over how he would explain to Shana what he'd done. When he woke the next morning, he was tired and still had no idea how to tell her. He stood in the shower relishing the warm soothing water as it ran over his tired body.

His mind went over all the possible ways to accomplish the unpleasant task ahead. He could call her, however the problem with cell phones was they often dropped calls. Or that person could just plain hang up if they didn't like the way the conversation was going. Then of course, he could simply talk to her in person. That was the best way, he knew, although he was unsure he could stand by and watch her walk away from him. However if he was there, he could try to stop her from leaving.

Kal finished his shower and dressed. He would drop Kalsha off at Sadie's and go to Shana's office as soon as he got to the hospital. If she didn't want to talk this morning, he would make sure she met him after work. He pulled into the employee parking lot and looked for her car. It wasn't there. Maybe she'd called in sick today.

He grabbed his cell and called her. There was no answer and the call went immediately to voicemail. This time he left a message for her to call him. He wanted to go right over to her apartment, but he was at the hospital and he had scheduled appointments to see patients until noon. He didn't have a choice, so he parked the car and went in.

Around one, he walked into Meg's office. His eyes glanced toward Shana's closed office door. "Is Shana gone for the rest of the day?" he asked.

Meg looked up and smiled. "Hello, Dr. Paxton. Shana will be out of the office for a week. She had some personal business to attend to back in Minneapolis."

"When did she leave?" he asked.

Taking Chances

"Early this morning. She's probably still in the air now, as we speak," Meg said looking at the clock.

"That's why I got her voicemail," he said, realizing why she hadn't answered her cell.

"Since she left on such short notice, I assumed something important must've happened back in Minneapolis causing her to leave right away."

"Probably."

"If she calls the office, do you want me to ask her to call you?" Meg asked, pen in hand and ready to take a message.

"No, that's okay, I'll try her cell again a little later. Thanks," Kal said and walked out of the office.

She must really be upset if she left to go back to Minnesota. He walked out to the parking lot to get his car and left, not sure if he was mad or scared. He headed home and called Sadie on the way.

"Kal?" Sadie questioned as she answered the phone.

"She left town and went back to Minnesota."

"She's probably scared. She's afraid you won't want her after you read the letter, so she went back home to the place where this all began."

"I'm going home, booking a flight to Minneapolis and packing."

"But how will you find her? Do you have any idea where to even look?" Sadie wondered.

"In the letter she mentioned, Tara, the counselor she worked with and the clinic name. I'll try calling there and keep calling her cell to see if she'll pick up."

"Hopefully she will."

"I'm going to try to get on the nonstop at five, so I can still get there tonight. Then I'll have to wait until tomorrow morning to go to the New Beginnings clinic where Tara works."

"Don't worry about Kalsha. She'll be fine with us."

"If you need anything for her you have the key to my house."

"I keep extra clothes here. You know I've got everything under control. Let me know if you'll be able to catch the evening flight. Call me from the airport."

"I will. Talk to you later."

Rose Marie Meuwissen

* * * *

Shana's connecting flight from Denver to Minneapolis left on time. She'd picked up a muffin and mocha coffee from Starbucks in the airport before boarding the plane and ate it as soon as the plane leveled off. Struggling to keep her eyes open and focused on the book she was trying to read, she finally gave in, closed her eyes and slept the rest of the flight to Minneapolis.

After landing, she picked up her rental car and drove to the Marriott Hotel by the airport and the Mall of America or MOA, as the locals refer to it, and checked in. She unpacked and lay down on the bed. Now what was she going to do, now that she was here?

She picked up her cell and this time she checked her messages. Kal had left a message! She listened to his voice saying how much he loved her and to please call him so they could meet somewhere to talk about the letter. She smiled. It was good to hear his voice. They couldn't meet though, because she wasn't in Phoenix. Nonetheless she actually did think he was right and they did need to talk in person. She would call him after she met with Tara. That was if she could get her courage up to call him back. She saved the message and called Tara.

"Tara?" Shana asked, not sure if it was her since she'd called the office number not her cell.

"Shana? Are you here?" Tara asked.

"Yes, I'm at the Airport Marriott. Where should we meet?"

"I won't be able to get out of here until about four. So how about five thirty at the California Grill at the MOA?"

"Isn't that place extremely pricey?" Shana asked, knowing her limited finances.

"I'm buying, so that's not an issue. And it'll be quiet there so we can talk."

"Okay. I'll see you there."

"Sorry, I have to see my next appointment, so we'll talk later."

Shana laid her cell down. She was relaxed, lying on the bed. Maybe she could simply close her eyes and rest for a little bit.

An hour later, she woke up. She must've been more tired than she thought. Or maybe it was only mental exhaustion. She knew she could

Taking Chances

sleep more but she wanted to check out the stores at the MOA before she met Tara, so she forced herself to get up and get moving.

The Mall of America was an enclosed metropolis of stores where you could shop until you drop and not have to deal with the winter weather outside. Granted it wasn't snowing, however it was cold. Especially after coming from Arizona.

As soon as she opened the door and walked in, she felt the warmth and comfort enfold her, a feeling that could only come from a place where you'd spent happy times. Years of memories. They were happy memories, yet they brought tears to her eyes. She remembered walking down the halls shopping with her mother. She shook her head to shake away the tears threatening to fall. They were good memories and she needed to remember them that way. Not with tears.

Unfortunately, she didn't have money to buy anything, especially after purchasing the air ticket and the hotel room. Fortunately looking was always free and most certainly always fun.

She started walking down the long halls of stores and stopped at the window of a children's clothing store. Little girl dresses were always so adorable and fun to look at. It was a holiday dress made out of red velvet and trimmed with green ribbons that caught her eye. She thought of Kalsha. It would look beautiful on her. In fact, she would look like a little princess.

Enthralled, she walked into the store to look at the dress up close. Shana picked up the dress on its hanger from the rack, touching the velvet gently and caressing it. Yes, this would be perfect for Kal's daughter. Kalsha was so perfect, silky blonde hair, and slightly pudgy cheeks that made you want to pinch them. This would be about the right size, a two.

She thought about Kalsha being two years old. Almost the same age she and Kal's child would have been. He must've met Kalsha's mother shortly after her and Kal met. This could easily have been a dress she would've bought for their child. She blinked her eyes to hold back the tears.

That was then and this was now. She took a deep breath to steady herself and her thoughts. She glanced at the sign above the dress rack advertising a half-price sale today. She could buy this dress for Kalsha

Rose Marie Meuwissen

as a Christmas present. Shana paid the cashier and walked out of the store with a beautiful holiday dress for Kalsha.

A beautiful child she wished was her daughter.

Chapter Fifteen

"Shana, it's been too long," Tara said as she hugged Shana.

"I've missed you," Shana answered, hugging her back while trying to keep a grasp on her package.

"I made a reservation so we should have a table shortly."

The hostess called Tara's name and they were ushered over to a table on the patio—at least that was what it was called even though it wasn't technically outside since they were inside the mall.

Tara ordered two glasses of white zinfandel wine for them and as soon as the waiter left she said, "So what happened to send you back to Minneapolis? Your email was extremely vague, but you knew that when you sent it."

"I don't even know where to start, Tara."

"I assume this is about Kal, so what happened?"

"Well, everything was going great. I think we had actually become a couple. He would even spend nights at my apartment."

"So what went wrong?" Tara prodded.

"We even spent Thanksgiving together, and I cooked dinner which turned out very good."

"That's great! I'm so happy to see you getting your life back to normal," Tara said, as the waiter set half-filled glasses of wine on the table, then said he would be back to get their order.

"And then he even kind of proposed."

"Kind of proposed? I've never heard of such a thing. What do you mean?"

"He said he wanted to spend the rest of his life with me and wanted to know how I felt about it."

"And I am assuming you said yes?"

"Yes."

"So what is the problem, then?"

"Monday at work, a coworker asked about my Thanksgiving and I said I spent it with Kal. I figured we were sort of engaged so it should be okay."

"I don't see anything wrong with that," Tara stated.

"That's not it, but what she said next. She asked if Kal brought his daughter," Shana confided.

"A daughter? And he never said anything to you?"

"No. I had no idea."

"Well, Kal having a child is not the end of the world, Shana."

"That's what I keep telling myself."

"What did you do? Did you confront him?"

"Yes, that very same day. I met him in the parking lot after work and asked him if he had a daughter. He said, 'Yes'."

"Did you ask him why he never told you before?"

"He said he wanted me to fall in love with him first."

"Well, I can understand that. Did you get to meet her?" Tara questioned.

"He picked her up and I met him at his house."

"What about his daughter?"

"She's a beautiful blonde two year old. Her name is Kalsha and she looks extremely like me when I was her age. It was a weird feeling and then all I could think about was mine and Kal's baby."

Tara stood up quickly and moved to sit next to Shana and put her arm around her shoulder. "I'm so sorry, Shana. It will be okay, you will get through this. Obviously he loves you or he wouldn't want to spend the rest of his life with you."

"Nonetheless I have to tell him what I did. I just have to. I can't accept his real proposal when he does propose, without telling him."

"He kept a big secret from you, too. So hopefully he will understand when you tell him. Does he know you left town?"

"I knew I had to tell him so I wrote it all down in a letter to give to him, however I accidentally left it in my office next to the inter office

Taking Chances

mail basket and Meg put it in the basket. So it was inter office mailed to Kal."

"You told him everything about the pregnancy?"

"Yes, I just wanted to get it all out there, so I wouldn't have anything to hide anymore. Do you think I shouldn't have?"

"It had to come out eventually. Telling him in person may have been best though. So did he call you after he read it?"

"Tara, that's why I'm here. I got so scared I didn't know what to do. I just wanted to get away and go home, so here I am."

"So he never called?" Tara asked.

"He left a message on my cell phone saying he wanted to talk, but I didn't call him back."

"Well, that's a very good sign. He must've read the letter and he still wants to talk to you. Yes, that is good."

"I'm so scared I'm going to lose him again. I wanted to do the right thing and tell him what I did. Do you think he'll be able to forgive me?"

"Hopefully if he loves you he'll be able to understand why you did what you did."

"You really think so?" Shana asked hopefully.

"There is always a chance. And you won't know unless you talk to him."

"Okay, I'll call him tomorrow after I go to the cemetery. I want to visit my Mom and Dad's grave. And have a talk with them about what's going on in my life. Then I'll talk to Kal."

"Now that's settled, let's order and you can tell me all the good things about your job and Phoenix."

"Yes, I'm hungry," Shana said. "And I want to show you what I bought."

After they ordered dinner, Shana took the dress out of her bag to show Tara. Shana's eyes glowed with pride as she held the dress up for Tara to see.

"It's beautiful. This is for Kal's little girl?" Tara asked.

"Yes, I simply couldn't resist. I wanted it for her. And just maybe she'll become my daughter, too, if Kal and I get married."

"Is the mother in the picture?" Tara asked.

"I did ask that, and he said she wasn't ready to be a mother at the time and had disappeared."

"Were they married?"

"I don't know. I do know he's single now."

After dinner, Shana went back to her hotel to try to get a good night's sleep. Her cell phone was on the charger and she turned it off because she didn't want to be disturbed, she wanted to sleep. If anyone called, specifically Kal, he could leave a message. She would call him in the afternoon after she got her courage up by talking to her mother. She was drained and she desperately needed sleep. As soon as her head hit the pillow, she fell asleep.

* * * *

Later that evening around ten o'clock, Kal's plane landed at the Minneapolis/St.Paul International Airport. Thankfully it hadn't been snowing. Knowing his luck, he would manage to be in Minneapolis for their first snow of the winter. Usually they had snow by now, but it had held off until after Thanksgiving and according to the weather reports there was a storm coming in probably tomorrow. He got his rental car, an SUV, just in case he needed it for the winter storm that was now forecast to be ten inches of the fluffy white stuff and drove to the airport Marriott hotel where he always stayed when he came back to Minneapolis.

After he got to his room, he tried calling Shana again, but her phone went straight to voicemail. She must have it turned off, he thought. Oh well, not anything he could do about it right now. He decided going to bed was the best thing to do because heaven only knew he needed a clear head when he talked to Shana tomorrow, so he needed to sleep.

The next morning after he showered and had a cup of coffee, Kal got on the Internet and googled the New Beginnings Clinic Shana had mentioned in her letter. He found the website listing and there was a Tara listed as a counselor. He wrote down the address and phone number. The office was not far from the hotel, so he decided to go over there instead of calling.

Taking Chances

He pulled out Shana's letter and reread it. His eyes watered after reading it. She'd been through so much and he was partly to blame for the break down she had. Their lives could have been so different. There wasn't anything he could do about the last two years, however there was definitely something he could do about the coming years for both of them. Not only did he need to forgive her but also he needed to have her forgive him. He had done some major praying and felt good about finally being able to make this whole situation right for all three of them.

Nonetheless first he had to find her.

* * * *

Kal waited in the parking lot of the Cedar Commons business building for half an hour after realizing they didn't open until nine in the morning. He wanted to give them an extra fifteen minutes to get situated before he went in. The weather was overcast, although it hadn't started snowing, yet it was definitely still coming according to the radio. He was most likely going to be stuck in Minneapolis for a few days if the storm was as bad as they were predicting. The Minneapolis airport was one of the best in the nation at keeping their runways open in snowstorms, however it did cause delays because no matter how good they were at the snow removal process, it took time to clear that much snow off the runways. Being stuck in Minneapolis might not be so bad, if he was able to spend the time with Shana.

Thirty minutes later, he walked into the office building, stopped at the receptionist desk and asked to speak with Tara Jennissy.

"Do you have an appointment, Sir?" the receptionist asked.

"No, but I need to talk to her."

"Can I tell her what it is concerning?" she asked.

"It's concerning Shana Madden," Kal stated, as if that should answer any and all questions concerning his visit to their office.

"If you'll please have a seat, I will tell her you are here, Sir," the receptionist informed him.

Kal took a seat in the waiting room. A few minutes later the receptionist returned, so he walked back up to the receptionist desk.

"She is in with a patient at the moment, but said if you can wait she will see you when she is done."

"Fine, I will wait," Kal said. He went back to his seat and picked up a magazine to read while he waited.

What seemed like an eternity to Kal, ended up being a half hour, until he was ushered into Tara's office.

Tara got up and walked over to shake hands with him. "Pleased to meet you, Mr. Paxton. What can I help you with?" she asked, motioning for him to have a seat as she returned to her chair behind her desk.

"I need to find Shana Madden and I think you may be able to help me."

"Why is that, Mr. Paxton?"

"I know you were and probably still are her counselor and possibly a friend. Shana and I need to talk but she got scared and went running back to Minneapolis. And probably came back to see you also."

"Anything between Shana and me is private and confidential. I can't reveal anything to you. But I am sure you already know that."

"She wrote me a letter about the chain of events that occurred after our one-night stand over two years ago. And then she took off running. I need to find her. And I need your help to do that."

"Why do you need to find her?"

"I need to explain my side of the story and why I did what I did."

"Will your explanation make her happy or push her over the edge again? She is my patient and of course I am concerned for her well-being."

"To be perfectly honest I am not sure. If she can forgive me I think we can have a happy life together."

"You truly believe that and being together is what you want?"

"Yes, I love her and I want the three of us to be a family."

"Well, why didn't you say that in the beginning? That makes a huge difference. You know I can't give out any information due to the doctor/patient confidentiality laws, but, when people are overwhelmed with a problem they don't know how to solve or what the outcome will be, the basic instinct is the urge to run away. And the place they generally run to is a place they feel some sense of security or a place that feels like home or is or was their home."

"This isn't helping. I don't know where her home was in Minneapolis. The address she gave me years ago was one she moved out of right after we met."

"But Minneapolis was her home, right? And that is where we are, right?"

"Yes, but you are talking in riddles. Minneapolis is a huge city."

"Another place people tend to go to is to see their parents."

"Her parents are dead."

"And if their parents are dead, they go to the cemetery."

"But they aren't really there so what good does that do?"

"There are a lot of people who go to grave sites and talk to dead parents, children, friends, etc."

"Great! How do I find out where her parents are buried?"

"Let's simply say for the record, a lot of men from that generation were in the military."

"The Fort Snelling V. A. Cemetery is just down the street, right?"

"Yes."

"Are you saying she is there?"

"I can't say, but you might start your search there and see what you find."

"Thanks, I think," Kal said and left. He knew the Fort Snelling V. A. Cemetery and he also knew how large it was. His parents were buried there. How would he ever find her father's head stone? There must be thousands of identical headstones in that cemetery, but at least it was a place to start looking for Shana.

Chapter Sixteen

Shana woke to a cold, dreary Minnesota morning that just shouted snowstorm with every gust of wind. It was coming and soon. She knew she would probably be spending at least one day watching large amounts of snow falling. Snowstorms could be fun if you didn't have to drive to work or shovel a driveway and had a toasty warm fireplace to sit by drinking hot chocolate with someone special. Like Kal. If only this whole thing worked out okay and he forgave her, but it was yet to be seen what his reaction had been to the letter. She kept reminding herself he'd at least called which was a good sign.

Thankfully, she brought her winter coat, hat and gloves since the temp had been dropping all night. She headed to the car and drove to a McDonalds a few blocks away to get a breakfast sandwich. Sitting at a table, she ate and thought about her life in Minneapolis with her parents. She'd grown up here, this was her home. She loved Minnesota, unfortunately not so much in the winter. Phoenix was more to her liking, especially in the winter, and she now had a life there, hopefully with Kal and Kalsha, too. Maybe they could come to Minnesota for a vacation in the summer. Minnesota was at its best in the summer with the lakes and all the water activities. Yes, if this all worked out she would talk to Kal about it, after all he was from Minnesota, too.

She picked up the Variety section of the Star Tribune newspaper on her table and glanced at what was going on in town. The Rockettes were in town performing at the new Mystic Lake Casino's Showroom. Macy's eighth floor Christmas display was the Nutcracker. She'd gone to see the Dayton's, now Macy's, display every year she lived in Minneapolis from the time she was a little girl with her parents up to when she left for Phoenix. One year she almost missed it but Tara had dragged her down there saying she needed it and seeing the Frosty display would be good therapy for her. So she went and she was glad she had.

Back in the car, she drove to the cemetery, which was only a few blocks away. She found the entrance gate and drove through the winding roads to where her parents were buried. Remembering exactly where they were wasn't the easiest since all the headstones were the same white vertical rectangular stones etched with names and dates.

Shana parked the car, buttoned up her coat, tied her scarf on tight, put her hat and gloves on, got out and slowly walked up to her parent's headstone markers.

She stood staring at the headstone bearing her mother and father's names, their birth and death dates. Visions of their faces and their times together floated through her mind. *God, how she missed them.* She wasn't so sure they would have been proud of what she'd done during those dark years yet she was sure they would've understood and that they still loved her, if that was even possible since they were dead.

"Mom, I simply needed to feel close to you so I had to come here. I know you aren't here but I hope you can hear me in heaven. I am not so proud of those years nonetheless I did the best I could and I tried to do the right thing at the end unfortunately it was too late. Hopefully, my daughter is with you and you are taking care of her for me. Kal did come looking for me. He tried to find me, however since I moved into your apartment, he couldn't find me. He is a good man, Mom. I love him and want to marry him. He has a daughter. I want to become a family with him and her and hopefully earn the position as her mother. She is beautiful, Mom. Looks exactly like me when I was little."

Shana shifted her feet as a large gust of wind blew from the North chilling her to the bone, making her shake from the cold. Nonetheless, she wasn't done so she continued.

"Dad, hope you are listening, too. I didn't mean to leave you out. I couldn't tell Kal at first what happened. I was afraid he wouldn't understand, and if our relationship didn't go anywhere, there wasn't a need to tell him. But now that it has, I had to tell him. I was scared, though, and couldn't tell him to his face so I wrote it all down in a letter and it was inter officed to him, which wasn't what I intended but it's the way it happened. Anyway, I just wanted you to know I'm okay, too. I have a good job again and a new life in Phoenix, where I might add it is much warmer than here! He called after he read the letter so I am assuming that is a good sign. I will call him when I am done here. Simply being here with both of you gives me courage and strength. And even though I am living in Phoenix now, my heart will always be in Minnesota with both of you and all the memories I have of our lives together. It's getting colder, I am getting colder, so I need to be going. I love you both and think about you often. Bye, Mom and Dad."

It was the freakiest thing but a flush of heat went through her body and the bone chilling cold was gone for a minute. Almost like a warm loving hug from her parents. Shana turned away and walked back to her car. She noticed an SUV parked behind her rental car. Someone else must be out here visiting a gravesite, too, on this cold winter day, she thought.

Just then, the door of the SUV opened and a man got out. He was wearing a long black wool dress coat and earmuffs. He walked deliberately towards her and she realized it was Kal.

Shana stopped dead in her tracks—tracks left in what once was light snow, but now was coming down in a raging, blowing fury.

"Shana," Kal said, stopping in front of her.

"Kal." Shana could hardly believe he was standing in front of her. "What are you doing here?"

"Looking for you."

"How on earth did you find me here, at the cemetery of all places?" she asked, completely dumfounded by his arrival.

"Let's simply say, I have my ways. And I was determined to find you."

"Yes, that is quite obvious." She tightened her coat around her as the wind kept blowing.

"I think we need to talk," Kal stated.

"Yes, we do, however it is extremely cold right here. Can we talk somewhere warm?" she asked, shivering.

"I'm sorry! My SUV is still running and warm, we can talk in there," Kal said moving closer and putting his arm around her to share some of his body heat. They walked to the SUV; Kal opened the door so Shana could get in then closed the door after she was inside. Kal walked around the SUV and got in the driver's seat. They both took off their gloves to warm their hands by the heat vents. Then the hat and earmuffs came off. Kal unbuttoned his coat and took it off, feeling more comfortable in his shirt. He was actually getting nervous about what he would say to her. He didn't want to say the wrong thing or to upset her. No, he wanted to clear the air about everything.

"Shana, I read the letter you wrote me. In fact, I have it in my pocket. I have reread it about ten times and each time it brings tears to my eyes."

"Kal, I am so sorry you got the letter through inter office mail. I meant to give it to you in person, unfortunately I set it down beside the inter office mail basket and Meg was just being her efficient self, saw it there with your name, put it in the basket and you know the rest. At that point there wasn't anything I could do."

"It's okay, Shana. You poured out your heart in that letter to me. I appreciate your honesty."

"Things could've been so different back then, if we both had done things differently." Shana was anxious now and became warm, so she took her coat off also.

"You already knew I tried to find you."

"Yes, but I obviously didn't know at the time. If you had even left me your business card, the whole thing may have turned out different."

"Shana, we can't change the past. We both took a crazy chance that night, for different reasons. I made a huge assumption on my part that you were on the pill."

"I have only had sex with my ex-husband and you, Kal. I wasn't sleeping with anyone so there wasn't any need to be on the pill."

"I'm not blaming you, Shana. I'm the guy and a doctor. I should've used a condom. I take full responsibility."

"Thank you. I have blamed myself for that part for a long time. If I hadn't had so many drinks it wouldn't have happened at all."

Kal could see relief wash over her. "I don't wish for one minute that that night didn't happen. We wouldn't be here today if it hadn't, and this is where I want to be right now. It was a bumpy road, that's for sure, however it led us here."

"I guess you're right. I want to be here right now with you. Nonetheless, you haven't said anything about the abortion. I have so much remorse and guilt about that day. I was in such a dark place and all alone. My choices were limited. I made a bad decision and tried to correct it, unfortunately it was too late. I have relived that day a million times in my mind, trying to make it have a different outcome. You have a daughter, but our daughter is gone." Shana cried. Tears she'd held back since talking to her parents at their gravesite.

Kal reached over, pulled her to him and kissed her cheek. His eyes were watering, too. "It's going to be alright," he said.

"Can you forgive me for what I did that day?" she asked.

"Shana, I forgive you. Don't ever doubt that. You need to forgive yourself."

"I have tried to and with your forgiveness I think I can get there."

"I need to tell you what my life path has been for the last couple of years since the night we met. I, too, have done some things I am not exactly proud of, yet they have actually turned out for the best for both of us. And there is something for which I will need your forgiveness, also."

Shana moved away from him wondering what he possibly could've done that she would need to forgive him. He obviously had something he needed to confess to her, though.

"Don't be afraid, Shana. It is going to be okay and we will get through this."

"So what is it you need to tell me?" she asked.

"I think we should go back to my hotel room and discuss it there instead of in this SUV, okay?"

Shana nodded and got out to get in her car. She followed him as he put his car in drive and headed out of the cemetery towards his hotel. The roads were quickly becoming snow covered as the storm was intensifying. There must've been at least an inch on the ground already. They drove carefully to the Marriott Hotel. The irony of the whole situation was even more obvious when she realized they were both staying at the same hotel. Hopefully it was a good omen meaning they were meant to be together.

They parked their cars and walked into the hotel. She followed him to his room, which was a suite with a separate living room, mini kitchen and fireplace. It was very nice and inviting, especially the fireplace. She took off her coat and laid it on a chair along with her purse. Kal did the same.

"Please have a seat." Kal pointed toward the couch. He would stand, because soon he would probably be pacing the floor while he told her what actually happened on that fateful day too many years ago. She sat down and he turned the gas fireplace on, knowing she was probably cold.

"So, what do you want to tell me?" she asked staring at him.

"Please bear with me on this. It is not an easy story to tell even though it is one I should've told you a while ago."

Shana was dumbfounded. She could not imagine what he was obviously so uncomfortable telling her.

"Shana, I want you to promise me you will at least listen to the whole story, before making any decisions about us. Okay?"

"What is this all about, Kal?" Shana asked, confused by his actions.

"I will tell you, but first, do you promise?"

"Yes. Now tell me."

"Okay here goes. That first night we met, I went to the bar on a lark. It had been a long time since I'd had a date or been with a woman. We met and I was immediately attracted to you. You were and still are so beautiful, and when you were dancing so sexy, first in front of me, then right up against my body, I had no willpower left. Of course, I didn't know if you'd even agree to let me go home with you at that point, but I knew I was definitely going to ask. I am not the kind of guy to have a one-night stand, in fact, I never had one before, and I, too, had more to drink than usual. When you agreed, I was ecstatic. We had and still have great chemistry. I had a great time however wasn't sure as what the proper protocol was, especially since I had to leave to catch an early flight out right away in the morning. I left the money because I couldn't take you to breakfast and felt I was ditching you at the last minute. It was apparent you drank a lot the night before and were still sound asleep. I didn't leave you my business card because believe it or not doctors don't usually carry them. I had a couple in the car but figured since I had your card I would call you when I got back."

"I was gone for a week, and when I got back I called your work but they said you were no longer employed there, and they were unable to give me any info about you. So if I assumed you knew you wouldn't be there anymore and still gave me your card that meant you didn't want to see me again. After another week went by, I thought I would try one more time and went to your apartment unfortunately someone else answered the door and said you'd moved. At that point, I gave up. I had no choice, you had disappeared."

"Is that it? Is that what you wanted to tell me?" Shana asked thinking she knew most of the story he'd just told her.

"No. Almost seven months later, my friend a fellow doctor, who works at an abortion clinic, called me at the last minute and asked me to take care of a couple patients who had appointments set up with him that day, because he had a family emergency. His mother had a stroke and he had to leave town unexpectedly. He knew how I felt about abortions but talked me into going in anyway. It's not that I am completely against abortions. In rare cases such as incest and rape, I agree it should be an option, however, one dealt with right away not months down the line."

"The first appointment at the clinic was a young girl who'd been raped by her uncle. That abortion I was okay with performing. The next one was a young woman age 30 who was approaching her 7th month. I read the file, including her story about why she wanted the abortion, and then read the name. It was your name—Shana Madden."

Chapter Seventeen

Shana stood up, her eyes darting wildly towards the door. "Oh my God!"

"Shana, sit back down and let me finish. You promised, remember," Kal said, willing her to sit back down.

"I don't know if I can listen to the rest," she said, visibly shaken, running her fingers rapidly through her hair.

"Sit down and take some deep breaths, Shana. It will be okay, just let me finish."

Shana reluctantly sat down and took deep breaths. Kal waited for her to relax a little before continuing.

"Shana, I did the math. I knew the odds of the baby being my child were high. I was livid. I had the nurse draw the baby's blood to run a DNA test. There was no way I was aborting that baby, so I had her sedate you so we could perform a C-section which would put the least amount of stress on the baby. The papers she had you sign were for the C-section and to give me all rights to the baby. I had the baby sent over to the pre-natal center at St. Francis Hospital for a couple of weeks and then I brought her home."

"You took my baby?" Shana shouted as her eyes flooded with tears. She stood up, lunged at him, pounding his chest with her fists. The anger she felt at that moment was overwhelming. After a few strikes she stopped and leaned against his chest, sobbing.

"Yes. Our baby, Shana." Shana felt Kal's arms go around her but she backed away, her eyes still glittering with more unshed tears.

"Do you have any idea what you put me through? And all for naught? If you hadn't sedated me, I would've cancelled the abortion and left the clinic." Shana sat back down on the couch.

"I was so angry with you for even wanting to abort our baby, I don't think I would've believed anything you said at the time," Kal said. "I wouldn't have trusted you." He walked over to the couch, sat down next to Shana and puller her into his arms.

"So she was alright? No complications?" Shana asked between sobs.

"Perfectly healthy."

"I feel so bad. I was so overwhelmed with worry at the time that there would be serious complications from the German measles and without medical insurance, I was at a total loss as to how I would be able to deal with it. It was such a struggle, when I got to the clinic I still wasn't sure and then I changed my mind, however it was too late." Shana cried uncontrollably.

"I did find out you changed your mind at the clinic, but it wasn't until weeks later when Jennifer, my nurse, talked to Kari, the nurse who stayed over-night with you that night at the clinic. Kari told Jennifer what you said when you woke up after the C-section. Jennifer contacted me because she thought I should know. I was still angry at the time though and simply disregarded it. I'm so sorry. I should have contacted you then, unfortunately, I was afraid of what your reaction would be. And I knew what I'd done was wrong. I didn't feel I could take the chance."

"I owe Kari a lot, she got me through that terrible night," Shana said between sobs. "I'm glad I told her. Especially now."

"Shortly after that fateful day, I got the job down in Phoenix and moved. I couldn't take care of Kalsha by myself, but luckily, Sadie, my sister lived in Phoenix and loves children. She has been a lifesaver for me. She loves Kalsha as if she were her own."

"Kalsha?"

"Yes, you met her. My daughter. She is our daughter," Kal admitted.

Taking Chances

Shana gasped, unable to believe the news that her baby was alive. "That's why she reminded me of my baby pictures. I thought it was odd she looked so much like me when I was her age."

"Every time I look at her, I see you, Shana. Can you forgive me for what I did?" Kal pleaded.

"I can't even believe this is happening. That this is even real. That I am her mother."

"It's all real and I am so sorry I had to deceive you to get us to where we are today. I love you Shana. To be honest I didn't think I could love you after that day at the clinic, and then when you ended up working at my hospital I was prepared to hate you," Kal admitted.

"I never hated you for what happened. That I got pregnant," Shana said, wiping at her tear-filled eyes.

"After I actually got to know you, there wasn't anything I didn't like except that fateful day at the clinic. I fought it, but I fell in love anyway."

"I love you, too. But can you forgive me?" Shana asked searching his eyes for an answer.

"Yes, I forgive you. We now have a chance to make this all right. Can you forgive me?" Kal asked.

"Yes! You have made me so happy today. I have been given another chance to be a mother. Also, let's make a pact now that we'll always be honest with each other. Okay?"

"Yes, honesty always," Kal said, feeling a huge weight being lifted from his shoulders. He tipped Shana's chin up so he could kiss her. She kissed him back. With the adrenalin high and racing through their bodies, the passion rose quickly and he carried her into the bedroom. He intended to make love to Shana, his woman, and for them to spend the night together. Kal kept his eyes on Shana as they both shed their clothes quickly. He pulled the quilt and covers back on the bed and within minutes their naked bodies were pressed together while his mouth devoured hers. His searching tongue finding haven in her warmth. He pulled Shana on top of his body so his searching lips and mouth could find her tantalizing pert breasts. He sucked on each one as she arched her body in pleasure. She straddled him and eased down on his rock hard shaft, bringing them both immense and immediate pleasure. He rolled over her so he was on top so he could control the rhythm, yet knew losing control was imminent, and he wouldn't last long with such intense passion pulsating between them. It was certain to be a long night filled with lovemaking until the wee hours of the night, with the snow falling outside the window covering the landscape in white while he covered Shana with all his love. This would be a night they would always remember for more reasons than one.

Shana woke the next morning lying naked in the king sized bed beside Kal. She remembered the long night with Kal and smiled. That was the best sex she'd ever had, but then it wasn't sex—it was making love, which probably made all the difference in the world.

She got up and peeked out the window curtain, and sure enough, it was still snowing. Her return flight wasn't until Sunday, but she wasn't sure on what day Kal's return flight was booked. He definitely wasn't leaving today she figured with the snow and all. She didn't doubt the airport would have to close down for a couple of hours to keep up with snowplowing the runways, and flights would most likely be delayed for at least a couple of hours. Maybe they could have some fun while they were in Minneapolis. She was still staring out the window watching the snow fall when Kal came up behind her and kissed her neck in an effort to coax her back to bed.

He proceeded to kiss her body everywhere, mixed with gentle caresses. Her body was on fire for him almost immediately. Soon they were making love again. Later, lying sated in each other's arms, the topic of food came up. Kal picked up the phone and called for room service to bring them breakfast. It arrived within the hour. Hot coffee and orange juice. A platter filled with fruit-strawberries, grapes, watermelon. Another platter was filled with scrambled eggs, bacon, sausage and hash browns. There was a pastry basket full of cinnamon rolls, croissants and muffins. They both sat down at the table devouring everything on their plates.

"I guess we missed supper last night," Kal teased.

"Yes, we did. When are you going back to Phoenix?" Shana asked.

"I thought we could go back together, so when is your return?"

"Sunday."

Taking Chances

"Then I will make mine for Sunday and see if we can be upgraded to First Class."

"Since we will be here for a few days, do you want to see the Rockettes at Mystic Lake?" Shana asked. "I saw an advertisement for the show at the Mall of America."

"I haven't been to Mystic Lake for years, except I did hear they have a new showroom. Sure, let's go."

"Did you ever go to see the Christmas display at Dayton's downtown store when you were little?" Shana asked, prodding and hoping he'd want to go.

"Yes, it was a yearly event. Do they still do it?"

"I saw it advertised in the paper. It's the Nutcracker story. But it's now the Macy's store."

"Let's go downtown on Friday. I haven't been down there for a while either. We can check it out and have dinner. Maybe they still have the Holly Dazzle lighted parade, too." Kal smiled as he saw Shana's face light up. He was going to spend the rest of his life making her smile and this was only the beginning.

Shana's cell phone rang and she checked to see who was calling. It was Tara. She didn't pick up in time though, and it went to voicemail. "I'm sure she is wondering if I'm okay. I'll call her after I shower."

"She probably wants to know if I found you because I went to visit her when I arrived in town. I figured she would be the only one who could help me find you."

"And did she?"

"You know she couldn't say much due to the doctor/patient confidentiality laws and all, however she did suggest in a roundabout way that I try the Fort Snelling V. A. Cemetery. I think I owe her, because I had no idea where to look, and I don't know if I would've found you if not for her."

Shana laughed. "That would be Tara. Always trying to get my life back on track one way or the other." She walked into the bathroom to shower, but Kal was right behind her.

"Care if I join you?" he asked pulling her into his arms.

"Not one bit!" Shana answered as Kal followed her into the shower and began kissing her wet lips.

177

After showering, Shana called Tara to fill her in on what had happened and planned a lunch the next day for the three of them at Doolittle's Woodfire Grill.

The next day they all arrived at noon at Doolittle's.

"Tara, good to see you," Kal said, shaking her hand.

"Glad everything worked out," Tara said as they followed the waiter to their table and were seated.

"Well, I for one definitely believe in miracles, now," Kal said.

"This is quite the story. Probably not many would believe it's even true," Tara said.

"It's not a story that needs to be told. Only a few know and it should stay that way," Kal said.

"Who knows?" Tara asked.

"My sister, Sadie, and her husband, Mac. And my nurse, Jennifer, who assisted me that day," Kal answered.

"And now Shana and myself. As far as I'm concerned it is doctor patient information and completely confidential," Tara said to ease Kal's nerves.

"Good," Kal replied, much relieved.

They ordered Doolittle's specialty, Wild Rice Soup, and Chicken sandwiches with waffle fries.

They ate. They talked. They laughed, as if they were good friends.

On Friday, Shana and Kal drove over to Mystic Lake Casino to try out the dinner buffet, which was ranked the top buffet in the Twin Cities. The buffet boasted prime rib, ham, turkey with all the fixings, an Italian, Asian, and Mexican aisle, salad bar with homemade soups, breads, and a dessert bar with everything baked on the premises. It was delicious. Shana tried her luck at the slot machines on a Viking Ship themed machine, winning a measly ten dollars nonetheless having fun in the process. Then they made their way to the Performing Concert Theater and found their reserved seats. The Rockettes performed their touring version of the Broadway Rockettes Christmas show to a sold out audience. Their performance was flawless, at least as far as Shana was concerned. The showroom was state of the art and every seat had a great view of the stage. Shana was on cloud nine. She was sharing this wonderful experience with Kal and she couldn't think of any place she'd rather be.

The Nutcracker exhibit at Macy's was on the list for Saturday. The only bad part was the long line to get in, yet in Shana's mind, it was absolutely worth it. Simply being in the old landmark Dayton's store in downtown Minneapolis brought back so many happy memories of times spent with her parents.

"Kalsha would love this," Kal said.

"Maybe we could bring her next year and make it a family tradition for us," Shana stated while leaning into Kal.

"I think that's a great idea, I'm all for it. I always liked Minneapolis at Christmas time," Kal agreed and gave her a quick kiss.

They grabbed dinner at Britt's Pub and then found a place to stand along Nicollet Avenue to watch the parade. The Holly Dazzle Parade was a winter parade with floats decked out in a Christmas light extravaganza. They purposely chose a spot outside of Starbucks so they could get some hot chocolate to keep them warm while watching the parade.

Sunday they boarded the plane back to Phoenix, with both of them seated in First Class. It had been a long time since Shana had been in First Class and she was going to enjoy every minute of it. Her nerves were on edge though because when they got back she was going to meet her daughter, Kalsha, not for the first time, however this time she was going to meet Kalsha as her mother. She was petrified yet excited. The flight attendant brought her a Baileys on the rocks. Shana took a sip hoping the Baileys would relax her a little and leaned back to enjoy the flight.

Kal leaned over and kissed her. "I love you," he said.

Shana smiled at him. "I love you, too."

Chapter Eighteen

It was a bright, sunny day in Phoenix when they landed, a drastic difference from the gray, overcast day they'd left behind in Minneapolis. Kal's car was at the airport, so it was an easy in and out process, especially since neither of them had checked bags.

Sadie was waiting at Kal's house with Kalsha. It was the longest ride of Shana's life. Thankfully, Sadie did not come out to meet them but waited inside. Shana needed this little bit of extra time to calm her nerves before meeting her daughter. She'd lost two precious years she could never get back. Making up for that lost time was foremost on her mind yet she knew she would have to go slowly at first to earn Kalsha's love. Although, there was no doubt in Shana's mind she would earn her daughter's affection. Kal had reassured her Kalsha was normally a very loving child anyway, so she would take to Shana in no time at all.

Kal opened the door to the house and Shana walked in with Kal close behind.

"Sadie, we're here," Kal yelled out, assuming Sadie and Kalsha were in the back of the house. Minutes later, he heard the patter of Kalsha's little shoes on the tile floor running towards him.

"Daddy," she said running into his outstretched arms.

"Oh, my beautiful baby girl! Daddy missed you!" He showered her with kisses and lifted her up. Turning her towards Shana, he said, "Do you remember Shana?"

Kalsha smiled a shy little smile and her eyes lit up. "Mommy? Pretty Mommy."

"I'll explain later," Kal said.

Taking Chances

Shana was taken back for a moment. Had he told Kalsha already she was her mother? It was a good sign if he felt good enough about their relationship to have already told Kalsha. She smiled back at this beautiful little girl who was hers and held her arms out. Kalsha reached for Shana and went into her waiting arms. Shana held her tightly to her chest for a heart-wrenching hug and a tear slipped down her cheek. "I love you," Shana said in Kalsha's ear.

Kalsha leaned back and said with a huge smile, "Love you." Then she kissed Shana on the lips as her daddy had taught her.

Sadie stood quietly in the background watching this monumental moment for these three very important people in her life. A long overdue moment. She couldn't have wished for a better outcome. Things must've went well in Minneapolis, with a quick glance to Shana's ring finger, she knew the only thing left was for Kal to seal the deal with the ring.

"Kal, Shana, glad to have you back," Sadie said. She walked up to Shana and gave her a quick hug. "I'm going to let you take over from here," she said to Shana who was still holding Kalsha. "Call me though if you need anything. I'm always willing to help out. I love that little girl, too." And with that, Sadie picked up her purse sitting by the door. "Oh, ask him about Kalsha's name." Then she was gone.

"Kal, what did she mean?"

"Oh, I named her for us. Kal for my name and the first part of your name Sha. Kalsha."

"I didn't put that together before, but I love her name, you chose well."

"She is a part of both us and so is her name."

* * * *

It was a busy week trying to mesh their two homes and lives together. Shana wasn't going to assume anything, as Kal had not actually proposed yet. She was pretty darn sure he would, but she wanted him to do it so she could make plans accordingly. Like giving notice on her condo.

She still had most of her clothes there, so she was there the following Friday after work, getting ready to go on a dinner date with

Kal. He only said they had things they still needed to discuss and since it had been such a crazy, hectic week, he wanted to treat her to a nice dinner. Besides, Sadie wanted Kalsha to spend the night.

Shana put on a little black dress that hugged her body, and spiked heel black shoes. Added a necklace, earrings, bracelet, and she was ready. He'd said to wear something nice, so she assumed they were going somewhere fancy.

Kal knocked at the door and let himself in. He had on a black suit. He looked so handsome it took her breath away.

"Ready, Beautiful?" he asked.

"I am," she said and picked up her purse.

In the car, Shana asked, "So, where are we going?"

"Sutter's Steak House."

"I've never been there," she stated.

"They have a fabulous reputation for great food and service. You'll like it. They even have great desserts."

Kal pulled up to the door of Sutter's Steak House and had the Vet valet parked. He walked around the car and took Shana's hand as she got out of the car and they walked in.

"Mr. Paxton, I have your table ready," the hostess said.

"Thank you." Kal followed her into the dining room to a corner table.

Shana was in awe of the ambiance of it all. The walls were lined with large oil paintings of the desert. Lights were low, and candlelight glowed from the tables. She felt like a princess in a fairy tale.

After they shared glasses of wine and dinner, they ordered dessert. The conversation had been light during the meal, only about work and plans for Christmas.

It was a perfect evening, she thought. The chocolate soufflé had been brought out directly from the oven to the table. It was warm, soft and melted in your mouth. Utterly delicious.

"The food was unbelievably good, Kal," Shana said. "It's been a perfect evening, thank you."

"Shana, I want us to have many evenings like this one. And many evenings at home with Kalsha. I want us to watch her grow into a beautiful young woman, like you. We both took a crazy chance that

Taking Chances

night in Minneapolis almost three years ago. We were both looking for something that was missing in our lives. The way we went about it may not have been the best, but it got us to where we are today. I think we were still looking for some missing piece to our lives, nonetheless when we met again, there was just something about you drawing me in and even though I fought it at first, I knew I wanted you. I wanted to spend the rest of my life with you. I wanted you to be my wife and Kalsha's mother. Please take another chance on us."

Kal's hand was actually shaking as it slid into his pocket to pull out the ring box. He got up, walked over to her side of the table, bent down on one knee, looked up into her sparkling amber eyes and said, "Shana, will you do me the honor of becoming my wife, for always?" He opened the box and held it out in front of her.

"Yes," Shana said, her voice breaking.

Kal took the ring out and slid it on her outstretched finger. He then stood pulling her up to stand against him as his lips met her more than willing lips to seal it with a kiss. He heard clapping in the background but continued kissing his future bride.

Epilogue

New Year's Eve

It had been a whirlwind few weeks planning a wedding for New Year's Eve. Kal wanted to go to Vegas and get married; however she truly wanted the long white dress and a real church wedding. Sadie agreed with Shana and they set out at record speed to get everything put together in time.

Sadie had finished helping Shana into her dress and veil. A beautiful ivory satin fitted dress with a flared bottom and adorned in sequins. Her hair was pulled up in an up-do with curls draping down in the back with the veil nestled snugly on top of the curls. It was time to take this once in a lifetime chance at happiness. She was going to do everything she could to make sure it was forever, too.

Kalsha was wearing the little red velvet dress she'd bought for her at the Mall of America back when she was in Minneapolis and she looked like a little doll. Kalsha was excited to carry the basket of roses down the aisle. Of course that was if she actually walked all the way down the aisle and there wasn't truly any hope she would drop roses along the way, still there was always a chance.

The music started then Sadie prompted Kalsha to begin her walk, and off she went, smiling and dropping roses along the way as she made her way down the aisle to where her daddy waited.

The music changed to the wedding march and Shana walked as slow as she could down the aisle to Kal and her daughter. It wasn't easy to go slow because she was in a hurry to get to them. Sadie took Kalsha

Taking Chances

from Kal, and Kal took Shana's hand as they walked over to where the pastor stood waiting.

The service was short with only a few friends and family joining them. Before she knew it, she was walking back down the aisle on Kal's arm as Mrs. Kal Paxton.

They stopped in the doorway to the outside garden for a photo and Kal took this opportunity to kiss his bride again.

"I love you. Thanks, for taking a chance again," he whispered into her ear.

"I love you, Kal," Shana whispered back. After a few pictures, Kal and Shana walked out to the garden patio where their friends, family and Kalsha were waiting to greet them.

Shana and Kal's journey had come full circle. With God's help, they were able to find each other again and open their hearts to take another chance on each other. They were now taking a chance on forever.

THE END

About the Author

Rose Marie Meuwissen, a first-generation Norwegian American born and raised in Minnesota, always tries to incorporate her Norwegian heritage into her writing. After receiving a BA in Marketing from Concordia University, a Masters in Creative Writing from Hamline University soon followed. Minnesota is still where she calls home.

She has been a member of Romance Writers of America (RWA) since 1995 and has attended multiple RWA National Conferences and Romantic Times Conventions. In 2012, she became co-founder of Romancing the Lakes of Minnesota, a local RWA Chapter in Minnesota.

She has traveled around the world, including Scandinavia, but still has many places to see, enjoys attending Scandinavian events, writing conferences and is usually busy writing Contemporary and Viking Time Travel Romances, Motorcycle Rally Screenplays, Nordic Cozy Murder Mysteries, WWII Nazi Occupation of Norway Historical fiction and Norwegian Traditions Children's Books.

Visit her at www.rosemariemeuwissen.com or www.realnorwegianseatlutefisk.com or www.romancingtherose.blogspot.com